Grace Ruby

Dearest Bonnie

May GRACE be your guide

♡

[signature]

2015

Grace Ruby

SILVER LAMB

ISBN: 1506144012
ISBN 13: 9781506144016

Dedicated to all of my introverted and extroverted friends...

Table of Contents

Part II

Part 1

One

Grace Ruby turned her delicate, worn teacup just a few degrees counter clockwise. There was a tiny, annoying chip that would catch her lip if she sipped her Earl Grey straight on. She never boiled the water, always there to lift the teakettle off the stove before the whistle's loud ascent. One measured tablespoon of canned milk, and one half-teaspoon of clover honey. Three slow stirs with her grandmother's antique miniature spoon and then the teabag was added. All of this was done at three o'clock in the afternoon, no sooner, no later. Grace liked ritual. She liked the way she could control certain moments in her day. Afternoon tea was one of her favorites. She inhaled the calm as she took a sip next to the tiny chip.

Placing the teacup onto its matching saucer, Grace put one foot in front of the other and glided over to her favorite chair. Thirteen steps, exactly, both hands on the saucer with eyes on the liquid's surface. Grace used this task to judge her aging steadiness—*so far so good.*

With the poise of her former youth, she lowered herself onto her tête-a-tête settee and placed the tea set on the doily-covered side table. Even though it was unladylike, Grace slipped off her ballet flats and extended her legs down the length of her side of the twinset settee. She crossed them at the ankles. Breathe, she thought, and observe.

'Control' and 'routine' were Grace Ruby's mantras. She whispered them under her breath over and over to match the ticking sounds of the front room's grandfather clock. Everything in the room was in its place: twentieth century curio cabinet filled with Lladro figurines tucked in the south corner, a small Birdseye maple dining room set pushed up against the north wall, and a Quoizel Transitional Tiffany floor lamp stood by the twinset settee. A lush, dusty rose patterned Persian rug sat perfectly aligned with all four walls. This is the room that gave Grace Ruby flawless peace. There was a solid, steady feel to the space. It wrapped around her shoulders like a favorite cashmere shawl.

Grace took a sip of cooling tea and settled her attention to the huge picture window on the northern side of her home. The heavy ruby colored drapes were open and the comforting reliability of the sun was sending beams of light to dance on the dust floating in the air.

"What craziness will I see today?" she spoke out loud to the attached empty matching seat stuck to her side like a conjoined invisible twin. "Am I safe from the world in here? Is the world safe from me?"

Tick, said the clock in agreement.

Grace picked up the Zhumell Mezzo opera glasses she kept tucked into the crux of her chaise's cushion. The metal rims always felt cold against her eye sockets, at first. There was an indifference to her voyeurism that she always had to overcome before relaxing and warming into her obsession.

Grace first pulled her attention to the distant horizon; just the usual, a slate-blue sliver of marine surrounding forest-green and butter-colored lumps of earth. The sky just a shade lighter than the ocean's blue. Grace recalled that today's forecast was for high winds. Tiny triangles of white were moving in slow motion from this distance, but their apexes were tilted severely.

She then tipped her head down slightly to soak in the comforting, never changing, view of the rooftops of her forward neighbors. Flat, severe, spired, shabby, elegant, deco, arts and crafts, Victorian, all crammed together like mismatched, broken crayons shoved back into the box.

She lowered the glasses and took another sip of tea, now for the street. This was Grace's entertainment. This was how she could fully dip into the water without getting wet. Grace Ruby brought the now warmed Zhumells back up to the bridge of her nose and licked a bit of honeyed tea from her lips.

The tourists, like busy little scavenger ants, were scouring for parking and easy walks. Each being with a fanny pack velcroed crookedly around each waist and a camera tugging at each neck. Those going down the hill bounced with excitement, those trudging back up lugged heavy bags filled with tourist trinkets and blocks of chocolate.

There were groups of first year university art students with sketch pads and pen boxes, military boys in uniform, young families with bulky strollers and diaper bags. There were skinny, tanned hikers with huge backpacks, and overdressed retirees wearing the wrong heels. There were walking tourist guides leading history buffs on hidden city gem expeditions, and hustlers getting their thieving ducks in a row. Every afternoon the parade never altered; different people, different ages, but all with similar intents.

Grace drew her attention to the north side of the street and smiled sadly, as she watched a young couple trying to walk down the sidewalk as one being. The girl's head and shoulder were pushed onto the boy's chest and her arm was wrapped around his middle like a second belt. They seemed to have so much attraction for each other, that they didn't even notice the incredible views to be had.

Grace felt a sudden tug in her chest. Observing lovers often did that to her. She had a cavernous hole she refused to fill. The beauty of time had allowed her to carefully build, intricate bridges across the missing parts of her life, but her secrets always screamed up from the chasm that she was not deserving—at least not of love. So at tea-time, Grace waded in to her own dirty clandestine.

She lowered the opera glasses and stood up. It was almost time, almost four.

Perfectly on cue, never failing, like the constant pass of the stars overhead, he appeared: tall, slender, well dressed—her forever obsession. Today he got out of his car slowly, shoulders drooping a bit. He patted the roof of his small import and paused for just the tiniest of moments before turning towards her window. Body straight, chin held high like in salute, he raised his arm and gave the tiniest of waves.

Over the years, Grace Ruby had gotten braver and braver. Every day she had inched closer to the thick pane of glass separating the moment, until one day she had been able to lift her hand and curve her fingers in a silent return gesture of a hello. This tryst of theirs had been going on for over forty years; a lifelong seduction of strangers.

Grace Ruby then turned from the window to calm her racing heart and headed to the study to write. Just of late, a different kind of story was pressing on her heart. She took up her pen…

Pouring winds rage down from the coastal redwoods
Raining wooden debris upon my joy like fairy dust
Running zigzag like the ocean's currents against the rocks
Free spirit blazing across the earth
Tiny squeals of exuberance echo across the expanse

When I, Grace Ruby, was a girl, I lived in a community of nature. Born into wealth, I lived as a pauper while my father acquired more money than the family could ever use. My cottage home was simple and modest; two bedrooms, a living area, two baths, and a huge kitchen, but it was my backyard that was amazing; over five hundred acres of natural wonder, a playground of giants, towering guard over a young girls imagination. Money could never buy the beauty that I immersed myself in. My playthings were the earthworms, millipedes, mollusks, and salamanders. All the things that only a child's eye, which subsisted close to the earth, could see. When I, Grace Ruby, was a girl, I was fully alive like the forest breathing behind my cottage.

~∿

I t was six o'clock, time for supper. Grace got up from her turn of the century writer's desk and pushed her chair in with precision. Tonight, was Italian night, perhaps a crab risotto or a small side of toasted raviolis dusted with aged Parmesan?

She went into her bedroom to change. Dark gray slacks and a deep lavender, long sleeve tunic for the damp weather that was sure to greet her on her way back home. Comfortable, practical shoes were the most important. Grace sat on her bed to pull on her Josef Seibel Sunflower sandals; orange of course, Grace loved orange. Lastly, Grace Ruby paused at her mirrored armoire to spritz a bit of Dior Cherie, just in case, then tied her long silver hair at the nape with a piece of ribbon from her dear departed grandmother's cache.

Grace slipped some twenties into her pants pocket, her house key, a small note pad, and her Monteverde One Touch ink ball pen. After an attempted mugging when she was in her thirties, Grace Ruby learned not to carry a purse. Luckily, because of her height and wiry strength, the small villain got away with nothing more than a bruised shin, and she, a pulled shoulder. From then on she never attached anything of value to her person while in view of the world.

"Eyes open and ears on alert," Grace whispered this outdoor mantra under her breath as she headed down the steep stairs of her hillside home.

Spring evenings were beautiful. The hidden jewel mini parks tended by the residents filled each block with scents of wild lilac, cedar, and juniper. A slight breeze brought up the brackish smell of dried iodine and salt. Someone was cooking bacon, perhaps for a BLT made with Early Girl tomatoes and Bibb lettuce. Grace slid her hands in her tunic pockets and inhaled the sensory memory to use later in her writings.

When you live in a hilly community, your body, especially your legs, stay in great shape. Grace knew to lean into the hill and bounce a bit off her toes to conserve energy and stay balanced. Her many years of ballet training made her more aware than most of how to harness the power of the lower extremities. The road she trekked up was packed as usual for a Friday, but with the grace of a dancer, and her name, Grace Ruby flowed in and out of the sidewalk traffic with nary a collision.

It was about a fifteen minute walk to her favorite Northern Italian trattoria. Grace had been dining there for two decades and was treated like family at each and every visit. Even on the most crowded of evenings Giovanni, the owner, would pull a tiny table from some back room and quickly drape the linens and set the silver, as if he was the famous close-up magician Slydini, himself.

"Buona sera bella signora," Giovanni whispered in Grace's ear as he pulled her into his Italian embrace of welcome. "The night is pushed away from the light of your smile."

Grace hugged him back a bit before pulling away to straighten her sleeves. Giovani had been flirting with his words for years. Grace lifted her finger to indicate, table for one, and Giovanni smiled wryly as he gestured for her to go before him.

Tonight, the small ristorante was filled to the brim. Many marvelous aromas were coming from the kitchen. Scribbled in florescent colored chalks were the evening's specials:

Spiedini Alla Romana
Ziti Arrabbiata
Mussels Basilico
Bistecca
and
Crostata di Mele (warm apple tart) for dessert

Grace sat down and asked for a glass of Pinot bianco with one ice cube. She brought her folded napkin to her nose and inhaled; a habit she had from staying at her grandmother's house. Ah, the aroma of formality along with the beauty of dining alone. No small talk, no scolding glances, no boredom from work details or family squabbles.

Grace crossed her legs at the ankles and looked around. Couples, every table filled with pairs: an ace-queen here, two deuces there, a jack—king, a pair of sixes—even, a couple of jokers. Grace noticed that Giovanni had graciously put only one place setting on her table. The wine came and Grace ordered the Ziti. She looked up once more, then pulled out her pen and notepad and began to write.

Why are your fingernails so soiled?
Earth child
Not all fragrance comes from the salt of the sea
Or the vanilla of the Ponderosa
Some of God's best fragrances come from the sweat of
Women's work in the home
Inhale the effort and be grateful

Dessert was lovely. Tart green apples piled high on a warmed almond cookie crust. Everything was cooled with a scoop of cinnamon gelato. Grace smiled. Everything was going along like it was supposed to. No strange surprises or sudden turn of events. Being in control in her home was one thing, but it was a completely different venture when out in public. Grace was beginning to breathe, knowing that she would soon be homeward bound.

"Mi scusi signora, ma questo e per te," Giovanni proclaimed, as he pulled an orange hibiscus from behind his back and presented it to the stunned Grace, "from the gentleman over there," he continued in English.

Grace turned her head to the entrance, but saw no one. She looked back at Giovanni but he merely shrugged his shoulders to deepen the mystery.

"Take it," the Italian insisted, while gently prying open Grace's clenched fist to receive. Slowly, finger by finger her palm began to release like the petals of a morning flower. She closed her eyes briefly and when she opened them a beautiful gift, the color of a sunset lay innocently in her palm, the exact orange of her sandals.

~⁹

Nine forty-five P.M., almost time for bed. Grace washed her teacup and spoon, and then dried them with a flour sack towel embroidered with a sea otter. She aligned the handle of the cup to exactly the same direction as the rest of the set, folded the towel in thirds, and then draped it over the oven door handle.

Before retiring to her bedroom, Grace crept into the darkened front room and up to the north facing window. As her eyes adjusted, she tenderly fiddled with the hibiscus propped up in a sterling vase with baby's breath from her stoop. When she returned from dinner, Grace had arranged the mystery gift and displayed it on her Chippendale oval end table, in the center of the window. Just in case.

Tonight the sky was unusually clear and bright. Still the tourists stumbled their way up and down the steep streets, but the sky above was lit with the brilliance of the universe's natural lights contrasting against the blackness.

Grace willed her eyes to look across the street's width and see if a light was on in the window a few feet below hers. All was dark and Grace breathed a sigh of relief. She looked down at the bloom, and watched as the petals closed up tight for the night, like her fist had been at the restaurant.

Two

As soon as her head hit the pillow, Grace Ruby fell down into a dream about her youth.

In this dream a torrential rain poured down at a steep angle. Young Grace was high upon a cliff, with her feet apart and firmly planted in a kind of defiance as the high winds propelled the deluge onto her ten-year-old body.

Grace had planned a simple razor clam digging morning. She had her narrow clam shovel and her favorite orange bucket. She had even pulled on an extra thick sweater when she had noticed the darkening morning sky before leaving her cottage home. But the day smelled like adventure and she had ignored her inner warning intuition and kept her eyes down on the squishy, pine needle covered path, avoiding Mother Nature's warning signs.

Capturing dinner was Grace's focus. She swung her bucket while looking for banana slugs along the walk and whistled to cover the sound of the wind.

The coastal redwoods lined her path like sentinels guarding the mysteries of the forest. Tall and ancient, the trunks stood firm as their limber branches waved and fluttered in the wind like human arms waving at a passing parade. Grace Ruby loved those trees and called them her brothers. She was an only child. She didn't have to look at the trees to know that they were there; like family, she was confident in their reliability.

Slip-sliding down the steep, bark covered path, Grace dug her dirty white Keds into the loose ground and used the clam shovel as a walking stick to help keep steady. How many times in her ten years had she traveled to the water's edge down this same secret trail?

As she leapt the last few feet to the sand, the darkening sky let out a low rumble, as if the world's stomach was growling and hungry to devour something tasty. Grace looked up for the first time that morning and furrowed her brow. That morning she somehow missed the sizzle of electricity hidden in the prelude of nasty weather.

No time for rain, Grace thought. Rain always soothed and lulled the elusive clams to sleep. Grace hurried to the water's edge, with her head down looking for the show.

Tamp, tamp, Grace Ruby used her feet and the handle of the shovel to draw a bigger dimple. Poised to plunge her trowel into the sand, drop to one knee to break the suction and scoop out the clam, Grace felt a giant drop of rain pound onto the top of her head. The sky then opened up and the ocean and the air above became as one.

No, no! Grace looked to the sea, watching the usually gentle waves build in size and ferocity. She stood for a moment, letting the rain water soak through her sweater and stretch the sleeves. Then she turned to run back up her secret path.

The narrow trail was slick with forest debris and patches of moss. She needed both hands to grab the roots and shards of shale. Grace turned her orange pail over and put it on her head to free up one of her hands.

Young Grace's face was red with anger. Rainy days meant staying inside and coloring, or some other boring activity like playing with dolls. The farther up she climbed, the hotter her temper rose. When she reached the summit, Grace Ruby threw her hands onto her hips and shouted down at her earthen playmate, "Fine! Be that way!"

But as soon as her words left her mouth, Grace Ruby caught a glimpse of red beneath the rim of her make-shift bucket hat. She turned just in time to see a 1957 Corvette Roadster sailing off the embankment next to Highway One, flipping once, before plummeting down onto the rocks below.

~_

Grace sat up straight in her bed with a start. At first she thought rain water ran down the sides of her face. Her heart pounded through her thin nightgown. As a tiny sliver of morning sunlight reached her, she realized that she was covered in sweat, not salty ocean water.

What had she been dreaming? The harder she tried to remember, the faster the memory ran away. Grace Ruby did not like dreaming. When a person dreams, they are out of control.

One must never be out of control!

Grace got up, washed her face and then went into the study to write.

Three

Towering blocks of wood
Stacked east then west then east
Nerves of a dancer en pointe
Steady, still, confident
All is right with the universe
Until
The wrong piece is pulled out
And life comes tumbling down

Eight A.M., time for breakfast. Grace pulled out a cantaloupe that she had chilling in the fridge. She sliced the round head of fruit in half, scooped out the pointy seeds, and then made four thick slices from each side.

Ding dong. *Yikes, they're early.*

"Good morning Grace, we know you're in there," sang Ethel Vogelzang's high pitchy voice, outside the front door. Today was Saturday. This was her Stairway Project Garden day.

"Give me ten more minutes. I will meet you there," Grace called back as she moved like a cat towards the front door.

She stood frozen with her ear pressed to the wood until their shuffling footsteps and whispered voices had faded away.

Grace inhaled relief and went back into the kitchen and resumed her work at the counter. She slid her knife under the flesh of a slice of cantaloupe and ate it with a fork from a small china plate. She refused to rush.

I am in control of my time.

After washing things up and putting them back exactly in the correct place, Grace changed into her gardening clothes. The sun was out this early spring day, so she chose stretchy, loose dungarees, and a long sleeved man's buttoned shirt.

After loading her gardening gloves, trowel, and Tommyco kneeling pad into her satchel, Grace stepped into the living area to check on her gift.

There it was, opened up to the world, proud and showy. Her orange hibiscus faced directly towards the home across the street. *Who would have sent this flower to my table?*

Most all of her sixty-two years, Grace had put up an impermeable force field of 'singleness' for the world to see. Never, for any reason, was she to allow herself to love or be loved. She put herself in a kind of loveless prison. She had friends, but kept them detached. She had some distant family left, but made little contact. She had her agent, her lawyer, her financial advisor, her fellow garden club members…but none were allowed too close. This steadfastness to an internal vow that she had made to herself some forty years earlier, almost made her feel proud. Almost.

～〜

Grace looked up from her thoughts and her heart shifted. There, across the street, beyond the oblivious tourists scurrying down the hill towards Ghirardelli Square was her tall, handsome neighbor holding something fuzzy and orange high above his head while looking right up into her window.

A kitten! Was that an orange kitten? Oh my, thought Grace Ruby, as she quickly retreated to the foyer.

~~

The Stairway Project Garden Club was something that her grandmother had belonged to. Grace fell into the program reluctantly when she moved into the house on Chestnut permanently after her grandmother's passing. Funded completely by donations, neighborhood residents took it upon themselves to cultivate and maintain the flora lining the steep step paths leading down to Bay Street. Folks took turns pulling weeds, picking up trash, and replanting. Over the years Grace began to love this citified return to nature.

"There she is," cried Ethel. "Over here!"

Today the group was working on repairing a broken sprinkler pipe. Ethel already had mud on her face, and two of the men were trying to stay balanced on the steep terrain as they dug a trench next to the pipeline. Grace slipped her gloves on, and then got on her knees to help pull away the loosened soil.

When Grace Ruby was down this close to the earth, some of her quirky inhibitions faded. Memories and feelings of how she was before the age of ten flowed up into her like roots, bringing water to the soul. The moist, woodsy aroma of decomposition, the hard work of the earthworms metamorphosing debris into loam, the quietness of having her ears next to the most solid foundation humans know, the planet…gardening was like a time machine pulling Grace Ruby back into happiness.

Noon, time for lunch, Grace Ruby sat shoulder to shoulder with Ethel on the top step of the Culebra Terrace staircase. It was Ethel's turn to pack lunch for the crew. In one of her Chinese take-out boxes, Grace found tiny finger sandwiches with the crusts cut off, filled with salmon, cream cheese, and thin slices of cucumber. In the other, a salad of baby kale, pine nuts, and dried cherries.

The Garden Club only did gourmet. It wasn't snobbery; it was just that their habitat was filled with unexceptionally great food.

"How's the latest novel coming along?" asked Ethel.

Grace paused for a moment. *People are so nosy and so pushy sometimes.*

"Well, it's not a novel."

"Then what is it?" Ethel asked, in between bites of salad.

How to answer this? What am I writing, anyway? This creativity burst is so different than anything I've ever created. I write fictional mysteries, for heaven's sake. I have no business prying into my own past.

"Well, it's a series of poems describing my life. A memoir, if you must," Grace answered after a bit.

"Oh I see," said Ethel. "Giving Sir Byron a rest, are you?"

"Something like that," Grace responded curtly.

A stiff breeze kicked up as Ethel stood up to pass out lemon squares to the rest of the crew for dessert.

Grace remained on the steps and looked out towards the bay for the millionth time, and still the beauty pushed at her heart.

"My life is a mystery," she whispered to no one. Grace stood up, tucked a few stray strands of hair back into her braid, and then swatted at the seat of her pants to remove the dust.

One P.M. Saturday, Grace Ruby's next stop was RG Coffee shop on Polk St. Normally she would have gone home to change and wash up, but today she felt looser; a bit undone.

Grace rummaged around in the bottom of her satchel to see if she had a note pad and pen tucked away, and she did. She ordered a cappuccino with steamed, in-house, homemade almond milk. Grace loved coffee but only allowed herself the bitter treat on Saturdays.

The barista knew Grace and smiled broadly at her favorite, steady customer. Grace tipped generously.

Cup in hand, Grace went a few doors down and ducked into a sanctuary of quiet, away from the electric buzz of pedestrian traffic; her home away from home, the RH Bookstore.

Nothing smelled like heaven to a writer more than an ancient, stuffy, tiny, bookshop. Grace inhaled and stared down at the thread-bare carpet as she moved to a petite table hidden behind the dusty bookcases and sat down to write.

Horror of horrors
Fear plummeting from the head through the gut
Like a runaway elevator
Slashed loose by that devil
Coincidence
Horror that buckles the knees
And turns the stomach
Stops the heart
And yanks the breath from the lungs
Horrific shift
While the rain pounds down
On the bucket
Without notice

Grace leaned back in her chair and looked around at the books facing out on the shelves. The proprietor was always kind enough to have her volumes facing her unofficial, small writing table: *Lord Byron and the Undertaker, Lord Byron and the Lady Augusta, Lord Byron and the Chinese Lecturer*. Those were some of the newest titles. There were so many now, that Grace Ruby had purposely lost count.

She had often been called "The Typical San Franciscan Recluse". Critics had both raved and torn apart her craft. She had fans all around the world and even a cynical *Chronicle Newspaper* columnist who liked to shred her books apart. Ironically all that did was increase sales.

Grace had money and fame, both of which she had no interest in. Her original money came from inherited 'old money', but now she was a multimillionaire by her own talent and work ethic. The fame that came with being a popular author frankly scared her. So Grace hired publicists to do the work of promotion while insisting they shelter her from any interaction with the public. This agreement was in place her whole writing career. Grace Ruby managed to feel blissfully alone in a forest of reading eyes, just like she wanted it.

"Excuse me, Miss."

A small voice along with a light tap on the shoulder made Grace Ruby turn around, slightly annoyed.

"What is it?" Grace answered, ready to drip with sarcasm. When she settled on the young girl's face, the color drained from Grace Ruby's cheeks; it was as if she had seen a ghost. There before her stood a vision from her past. A doppelganger of someone she once knew.

"My mother and I were wondering if you would sign this book, please," asked the girl.

She was probably just six with snow white, straight, long hair. Her skin was translucent and her eyes pale rose, like an albino. Grace saw that she had child's sunglasses dangling from a cord wrapped around her neck.

This can't be. This is so odd. Grace took the opened book with trembling hands, never taking her eyes off the child's face.

"Thank you, Miss," the girl said politely as her blood red lips formed the words.

Grace took the pen she already had in her hand and scribbled her signature on the inside of the front cover. When Grace looked down, the writing looked like chicken scratch autographed by an insane person. The girl took it and left with her mother.

Sick, she felt sick. A revulsion so strong washed over her that Grace leapt up, spilling her chair as she lunged over to the small restroom in the back of the store. Up came the finger sandwiches and pieces of kale that now resembled seaweed. Grace was on her knees dredging up the past in the most surreal way possible.

The walk back home was arduous. Grace's stomach felt better, but it was the shock of seeing that little girl that kept her heart beating erratically. Why did she have such a reaction to a perfect, sweet stranger? She thought she knew the answer, but she wasn't ready to go there yet.

Grace turned her attention to the store fronts she passed on her way back up the hill. So many little boutiques, tea shops, sushi spots, pancake houses; all thriving behind Victorian and Deco store fronts. New lives housed in old buildings.

Grace herself felt like an old life housed in an old body. She felt safe in her routine, comfortable, in control. But for the last few weeks something had been itching from the inside, like a tiny mosquito bite that can't be easily reached. Perhaps it was the memoir she was attempting to write. Every poem that came to her was like lifting the lid on a boiling kettle of soup, higher and higher, making memory steam fill her senses.

Maybe it was just age and time. Did she have regrets about her reclusive choices? Was she deserving of love? *Crazy, just crazy,* thought Grace as she pulled her satchel full of gardening tools, and writing implements closer to her heart.

Ah, the safety of home. Grace clicked the front door shut and locked the dead bolt. No tea today. The sour coffee taste still lingered in her mouth.

Grace put away her gardening tools and retreated to the bathroom to take a hot, steaming shower. She brought a fresh bar of lemon verbena soap to her nose and inhaled her favorite bath scent as the water spray washed off her shaky day.

A nap was what she needed. Grace loved naps. Naps generated good thoughts. Grace tucked her towel dried hair in a casual French twist and slipped in between her Mulberry silk sheets to think about her neighborly obsession.

Four

June 1, 1977 was the first day that Grace Ruby had noticed her dashing neighbor. Grace was twenty-five and had been living in her deceased grandmother's home for a year. June 1 was also the date that her very first manuscript, *Lord Byron and the Bee's Nest*, was sold to a publisher.

That morning, Grace's agent had barged in with a bottle of champagne to celebrate. Brash, yet the best in the business, Carla Lingam was beyond ecstatic about her severely withdrawn client's success. She hugged the young writer and then coaxed Grace over to the bay window to make a toast to the city. It was then that both women had spotted the wiry young man with the ponytail, dressed in a black fitted suit, stepping out of his pale yellow 450SL Mercedes.

"Wow, nice view," Carla had offered.

At first Grace had thought Carla meant the bay. But then her eyes had gone down to the street and caught a glimpse of the man as he patted the hood of his car, then disappeared into the lower entrance of the building across from hers.

No, no thought Grace, *I won't allow myself this feeling.*

What feeling was it? *Attraction, of course.* Grace had backed away from the window... for the next thirty years.

*I*t was like that. Grace Ruby would catch a glimpse of her neighbor sporadically at first, then at certain strict times over the decades.

She watched his dating years, bringing young women home at late hours, wild looking girls with neon skirts and Farrah Fawcett hair.

She watched his early courtship with his future wife. How cute she was, tiny and petite.

She watched as his hair got shorter and his financial successes showed with each sports car purchase. She watched as his young family grew by two. She watched the beauty of their love. She cherished his life. The idea and vision of it was precious to her.

Once in a while she would spot the four of them out and about. During those times, Grace would hide behind a bookcase, or shopping aisle, or crowd of tourists, and observe. It was like she was young again, roaming the woods next to her cottage home, on the lookout for a rare sighting of a beautiful, native bird.

She would see him nestle the neck of his baby girl. Or hold hands with his wife and son as they crossed a busy intersection. The observations were quick, but the scenes etched in her mind as something unattainably solid.

Never, ever, did she let him see this interest, because there was no interest, there could never be any interest. Grace could never love him, or them, or anyone else. Everything and everyone that Grace Ruby loved died. This beautiful bird and his family that nested across from her could never be touched by anything but a passing coincidence. Grace lived her years in isolation as a punishment for her crimes; that was just the way it had to be. It had to.

Five

When you are small
And your sturdy wall
Crumbles before you
A shift of direction
Incurs an infection
And cracks open a darkness

You no longer stand
On rock solid land
Emotions become erratic

A reckless crazy
Makes life hazy
And the new you becomes dangerous

Grace laid the pad and pen next to her bed on the nightstand and got up from resting. Saturdays were always a little off for her. The routines Grace loved were sometimes altered on the weekends and it threw her off of her normal, controlled schedule.

She sat on the edge of her bed and listened. The grandfather's clock in the front room was ticking and straining to chime the hour. It was strange how most of the time she never heard it. But then, when her mind was on a certain awareness level, the sound was deafening.

Knock, knock, knock!

Grace jumped from her thoughts, startled.

Who could that be?

Saturdays were usually quiet and steady.

Grace Ruby pulled on her Gingerlily ivory silk dressing gown and headed to the front door. She was not expecting anyone. *This was Saturday, for heaven's sake.*

The knocking had been thunderous and quick. There was no sound now, so Grace approached the peephole quietly. She peered out and saw no one. Wary, she backed away, holding her breath and ignoring the grandfather's clock ticking.

With caution she turned the knob and looked out. Nothing. She was about to shut the door when something caught her eye on the top step. A basket. A picnic type basket with a lid.

The late afternoon fog rolled in over her rooftop, making the lighting a bit disjointed and eerie as Grace Ruby approached the unusual bundle. Mostly she received packages from publishers or book club fans. This was different, just a plain, brown basket with an orange bow attached to the handle.

Grace Ruby leaned over the railing to see if she could catch a glimpse of the deliverer. But there was no one. She squatted down to gather the basket, but it moved a bit. Grace jumped, heart pounding.

Oh no, what could this be, a snake, a joke, something dangerous, perhaps?

The basket remained still, so Grace grasped it firmly by the handle and took it into the house. She placed it on the kitchen counter.

The orange bow on the top had been secured so tightly that Grace had to use scissors to cut it off. When she did, the basket moved once more.

Grace Ruby was an introvert, but she was brave. Introverts had to be brave to navigate the world, often alone, by choice. She held her breath, lifted the lid and stepped back a bit, just in case.

As she peered over the rim, there in the bottom of the basket sat a little orange kitten, perfectly still, looking up at her with big, golden green eyes.

Oh no, this will not do!

In all the years she had lived in her San Francisco home, she had never taken in a pet.

Wasn't she allergic to cats, anyway?

As that thought was going through Grace's mind, she and the kitten never broke eye contact.

Grace's cardinal rule was not to love anyone. This had included animals.

Over the years friends had tried to get her to get a dog, or a fish tank, something living to care for. But Grace had refused, and no one knew why but her.

It wasn't because she didn't love animals, because she did. Animals and all of God's creatures were her life when she had lived and played beneath her giant, coastal redwood brothers as a girl. But life had changed in an instant, and Grace had to adhere to the oath that she had made to herself years and years ago: Do not love, and do not let love find you.

The kitten waited patiently to see if Grace Ruby would finally break her oath and release the prison bars of her emotional captivity. The cat blinked and so did Grace Ruby.

What to do, what to do? Grace's mind raced. *Is our SF SPCA open on Saturdays? Would that pet store on Polk take in a kitten?*

Grace could not imagine cat food, bowls, furniture scratching…*a kitty litter box? What if it bites someone, or hisses at me? Who will*

*take care of it when I have to do perfunctory book signings? What about the
cat hair, the lap kneading, the smell?*

Then the little creature opened its mouth and made the sweet-
est sound that Grace had ever heard and her heart leapt in her
chest.

⁓⁓

It wasn't until later, after Grace had laid her hand flat in the basket and the tiny orange baby had crawled onto it, and they had
snuggled on her tête-a-tête settee to get to know one another that
Grace thought to look in the basket for a hint of who had sent it.

The kitten had fallen asleep after lapping up a saucer (taken
from her teacup collection) of warmed milk. Grace took the kitten
into the bedroom and tucked it into a plush towel and laid it on
the foot of her bed.

In the kitchen, the basket sat there innocently, oblivious of the
momentous change it had delivered to the older woman's heart.

"What's this?" Grace asked. It didn't sound crazy to talk out
loud now that there was something else living with her.

Down below the little rag that covered the bottom of the basket
was an envelope. Grace felt her pulse quicken. She looked around
for her glasses, and then took it into the front room to open it.

Inside she found a handwritten note. It said:

**Rapunzel, Rapunzel let down your hair,
So that I may climb the golden stair.**

And a gift card to Pet Central.

Six

race pulled on some slacks, a tee, and her orange sandals. Then she went back to her closet and found her light orange windbreaker and put that on as well.

After checking on the kitten to make sure it was still asleep, Grace hurried down to the pet store. She walked the back trails to avoid the foot traffic.

Why am I wearing all of this orange? Am I trying to give off a signal?

As she stumbled a bit over a root in the ground, Grace took a moment to do an inventory of how she was feeling.

The morning had started out well, nice and routine. The Garden Club work had felt good and there weren't too many interactions with the members. This, Grace liked. But then, the pale little girl from the bookstore had startled her. More than startled, the child had scared her. So strange how an interaction with someone could shove you instantly back into the past. A past that was secret and dark.

Then there was the gift, a basket with a life inside. Grace had a good idea who had sent it.

Hadn't I seen my neighbor holding the very same kitten high above his head earlier? But why did he assume that I would want such a complicated present? And was he the one who gave me the orange hibiscus? More importantly, was this why I had pulled on my orange windbreaker?

"May I help you?" asked the pet store clerk pulling Grace out of her thoughts.

"I hope so," answered Grace and together they gathered the supplies for Grace Ruby's new life's direction.

~)

T en P.M., home in bed with a little orange ball of fur curled up in next to Grace's head.

She had hurried home with her supplies, but had paused for a few seconds down below her neighbor's three-story home, just in case he was watching for her.

How crazy was that? thought Grace.

The little kitten was a boy. The pet shop cashier had told Grace what to look for. Of course, she named him Lord Byron, the Baron; BB for short.

BB reminded Grace of the cat that her mother had given her after the accident to try and pull Grace out of her depression. Now that she looked back upon it, she could see her mother's good intentions, but at the time all Grace did was cry.

Seven

Red car, red car, wheels spinning round
Why, you look so familiar
Lying upside down

Do I know you?
Do I do?
This angle seems so mad

Do you live at our house?
Don't you belong?
To my dad?

~

I knew my father as well as any young girl did in the early sixties. I knew he had an important job for which he needed to go to the city. I knew that he wore blue gray suits like President Kennedy. I knew he loved Old Spice aftershave, and that he kept two handkerchiefs, one in his suit pocket and one in his trousers. I knew my father was obsessed with the Vietnam War and Giant's baseball. I knew he had both Willie Mays and Filipe Alou's rookie baseball cards. I knew he liked dogs but not cats, baked potatoes but not mashed, pipes but not cigars.

What I wasn't quite sure of was whether he loved me or not. Oh sure, he brought me toys and books, ant farms and bug nets, pretty sweaters and sneakers. He came to my school functions when he could, and sometimes he even tucked me in. But, I could not quite recall him ever saying the words 'I love you', out loud.

This is what I was thinking as I ran through my silent coastal redwood brothers swaying high up in the swirling storm. The trees seemed to be propelling me down the trail, flailing their branch arms in a panicked frenzy. I had lost the clam shovel on the way and had thrown my orange pail into the Gold Back ferns that lined the path. I actually felt I had stopped breathing. In my mind, if I could just hold my breath all the way home, everything would be okay.

The rain was coming down even heavier now and my heart fell to the lowest point of my body as I raced up the empty driveway. No red Corvette Roadster in the carport. Not enough air in my lungs to scream. I just dropped to my knees and collapsed.

~

The next few days were a blur. I remember bits and pieces of the police visit and the trip to the coroner's office. My grandmother came to stay, but I couldn't recall for how long. There were casseroles and pound cake, as neighbors and my parent's Bridge Club friends poured in with flowers and stories and long hugs.

Someone had even gone down to the wreck site and found a handkerchief snagged on a craggy piece of shale below the cliff. I snuck into my mother's bedroom and retrieved it, then placed it under my pillow. It smelled like daddy, it smelled like Old Spice.

But then the whispers started, grownup talk, the kind that stops when young ears enter the room. I could see another type of grief creep across my mother's face as the quiet voices droned on and on. Almost overnight it looked like Mother had aged ten years.

What was going on? What else could possibly be wrong? I wondered as I pressed my ear to the often closed doors.

Silver Lamb

The last time I had spent time with my father was a few days before the accident. It was late on Sunday and I wasn't tired. During the summer, I didn't have a set bed time. My mother often went to sleep early and my father and I would stay up and watch The Ed Sullivan Show and The Real McCoys.

This particular Sunday, my father had lit his pipe and told me to go get both boxes of the Jenga-like game he called Sidan. Father had acquired the games of stacking blocks on one of his work trips.

For as long as I could remember, the two of us had attempted to stack the tallest Sidan tower in the entire world. The highest we had gotten was a box and a half. Most of the time, after a couple of tense attempts, we would just play a regular one box game.

I held my breath as I tried to remove a block without the tower tumbling to the table.

"You must keep entirely steady, Ruby Gem," my father would instruct with a soothing voice. "Never let anything rattle you."

Sometimes, he had even wrapped his hand around my hand to help steady my grip after my decision had been made.

"Slowly. Slowly. Hold your breath and never give in."

CRASH!

Down tumbled all we had built; down, down, down. Everything came down after the crash.

Eight

Seven A.M., *what was that noise?* It sounded as if Grace had her ear on the tarmac while a jet plane was taking off. *So loud!*

Slowly Grace's awareness became clearer. When she tried to move her head she realized where the sound was coming from, BB, her new breath of life, was tangled up cozily in Grace's long hair, purring directly into her ear, and Grace's pen and memoir were scattered across the covers.

"Wake up, wake up," the kitten was saying, "I'm hungry."

Grace was hungry too. She hadn't eaten since lunch on the steps. Grace picked up the kitten and went into the kitchen. She sprinkled a little kitten chow on a plate for BB and scrambled some eggs for herself.

Today was Sunday, church day. For forty years Grace Ruby had not missed a service. The unusual thing was that Grace did not belong to any one church. There were hundreds of churches in the Bay Area and Grace made her way to visit all of them, many more than once. She considered herself a seeker and a sampler. Grace liked the freedom of anonymity she attached to her personality. She could just slip in without notice and leave with a different perspective.

Many of the services in San Francisco were in different languages. Those sermons that she could not understand were often the most enlightening.

Her debate with God was long and unending. She had so many questions. Traveling from church to church, from one religion to another, Grace had found fundamental answers that just brought up more questions. She had learned that questions propelled her forward and answers often stopped the momentum. So she would pull up her city map to select her next classroom and slip into a back pew, or bench, or rug square on the floor and continue her search for something; really she wasn't sure what it was, she just knew she was still hungry after all the years of Sunday seeking.

Grace took one more bite of eggs and then scrubbed her plate clean in the sink.

"Meow," said BB with a tiny voice. Grace bent down to pick him up and snuggled him to her chest. He answered her affection with his surprisingly loud purr. After church, she would take her new family member back to the pet store to have the in-house veterinarian check his health and offer more tips for his care. For now, Grace felt the overwhelming desire to start a routine.

Now that he was fed, Grace took the kitten to his litter box and he immediately went to town. Grace then set up a retrieval and disposal area, and added the pet neutralizing odor spray that the pet store clerk had suggested. As she went through the house rearranging for her kitty, little BB followed under her feet. She learned that she had to move carefully to avoid stepping on him.

"Meow."

Grace obediently bent down to pick him up and cuddle him again after she was satisfied with the alterations of her home. He smelled so sweet and felt so soft, and he was orange, her favorite color. *What a coincidence that was. Or was it?*

Grace moved into the front room with the kitten tucked in the crook of an arm. With her free hand she took her Zhumell Mezzo opera glasses and sat down at her tête-a-tête settee. BB wiggled out of her grasp and clawed up and over to the empty attached chair, then curled up in a ball.

Hyde Street was as busy as always on a Sunday. There were a few locals dressed for church, but mostly families of tourists with loud Hawaiian shirts and flip-flops on their feet.

Grace moved her gaze past the orange hibiscus that was slowly opening to the new day in front of her bay window, and risked a direct look into her neighbor's awning-covered terrace. The flowers that his wife had tended were long dead. All that remained were empty terracotta pots and some overgrown needle point ivy. The home's heavy drapes were closed, and when Grace focused the opera glasses even closer, she could see that he had taken down one of the two patio chairs that had been there forever.

How heartbreaking, thought Grace as she got up to get dressed for church, *tragedy is everywhere.*

Nine

How could you deceive all that was sacred?
In the heart of a family
We were your world
You were ours
Now that world has been shaken and broken and crumbled into
A million bitter pieces
Of anger, hurt,
And unbearable, emotional trauma

~~~

Because of BB, Grace picked the closest church to her home, the Norwegian Seamen church on Hyde. Today's sermon was completely in Norwegian. Grace had slipped in, thankfully, without any notice and sat in the farthest corner of the back pew. She let the words of the speaker flow around her as she gleamed all the meaning that she could. It seemed to her that clemency was the subject. Grace closed her eyes and contemplated clemency or forgiveness. Then she discreetly took her pen and wrote more of her memoir.

Grace Ruby

The day ten-year-old me finally got ahold of a sentence drifting out of an open window of our cottage, I had been sitting quietly on the front porch steps. I was petting an orange tabby cat that my mother had picked up from the rescue center. The cat was sweet and docile and loved to be held. I was never allowed a cat when my father was alive.

My Auntie Mae, my mother's sister, had been drinking and was talking louder than normal. Mother kept shushing her to no avail.

"I never liked him, I tell ya, I never once liked him," slurred Mae.

"Quiet now, Grace Ruby will hear," whispered mother loudly.

"You two married too soon, and too quickly! Think of all the times he went away, 'for work' and never really said what he was doing," Mae went on. "And what about Jennifer Hexel, remember her?"

I put down the cat and scooted over to under the sill. My stomach suddenly knotted up as the conversation went on. Who was Jennifer Hexel?

"We don't know anything," mother rebutted firmly. "The detectives are just now figuring out who she was."

"Well, there was a woman in his car. Did he tell you about her? Did you know that he drove women around in his car? And what about what that waitress said from the coffee shop in Mill Valley? She had seen them together so often that she thought she was his wife!" Mae was almost shouting now. "She thought YOU died in the crash!"

I couldn't listen to anymore. I got up and knocked over the rocker on the front porch. I ran and ran as fast as my legs could take me. Away I went, away from my formerly warm cottage home, a home that had turned in an instant to a house of horrors. Faster and faster I went tearing down my childhood trail, through my family of trees, and towards my other mother...Mother Ocean.

When my lungs had given out, I found myself on the northern edge of Muir Beach by Redwood Creek. I picked up a long stick and dragged it through the late afternoon, wet sand. Harder and harder I pressed down as the anger I felt boiled up.

Who was it that died alongside my father? Why did it have to be a lady?

I thought back to the first visit from the police.

Hadn't they said something about another person in the car?

At the time, I thought there must have been two cars in the accident. It was raining so hard, maybe I had not seen the other car.

I had that darn clam bucket on my head. Why didn't I crawl down the ravine to help, anyway? I could have given...what was it called? CPR or something and saved Daddy. But no, I got scared and ran away like a big baby. If I had only gone down to see, I could tell Mother that no one but Daddy was in the car.

Snap! The stick I had been pushing into the sandy ground fractured, and so did my childhood.

Ten

"Amen," the Norwegian pastor said in English at the end of the service. Grace Ruby put down her pen. The aroma of waffles was coming in from the parlor in the back of the church. The few times she had attended their services Grace would go in and enjoy a Norwegian waffle with lingonberry jam. Then she would sit by the big window, facing a slightly different view than her own at home, and write a chapter of *Lord Byron*.

Today, she felt something different.

What is it? A pressing desire to go home, not because of my introverted tendencies, but because I have someone depending on me…baby BB…what is happening?

Grace was beginning to break her own vow of never loving anyone. She felt her stomach knot up as she headed back to her home.

What if I lose the kitten or it gets run over…or, what if I kill it somehow?

Grace was in a full panic now. Sweat beaded on her forehead and she began to shake internally as anxiety took over.

What am I doing, letting love into my heart?

Grace hurried up the steps leading to her home on shaky legs.

She threw open the front door and there sitting patiently was her new, living little buddy, BB. As she closed the door, Grace gasped for an inhaled breath while BB waited tolerantly for her new owner to calm herself. Then the kitty simply walked over and started rubbing and winding between her ankles; the more he rubbed and the louder he purred, the more Grace's heart slowed from its panicked pace.

"He's alive," Grace whispered, and then immediately realized how crazy that sounded. Of course he was fine; she had only left for an hour or so.

Grace reached down and picked up the little creature, then nuzzled him into her neck and under her chin. Melting, was the best way to describe what the rush of anxious adrenaline leaving her body felt like, melting. From her head to the tips of her toes, she could feel herself dissolving, like ice cream on a hot summer's day, or the wax off one of her grandmother's tapers. It was more than that. It was the vow. The vow of unloving was talking to her. It seemed to be saying, *enough is enough. Forty or so years is enough time in prison; let's let you out in the yard a bit. Let's let you have a little sunshine and see how it goes. Let's take it slow.*

"Purr," answered BB when he felt Grace had finished her internal dialogue.

Maybe love between things can be quite OK.

"Purr."

Eleven

Higher and higher goes the Sidan stack
Intricate and complicated
Like adolescence

~❦~

Three-thirty P.M., 1963, I flew out of Mrs. Snapin's science class door the minute the bell rang. I was in trouble once again. I hated school, I hated everything. Bill Macken had been teasing me; calling me 'bastard baby' and a 'rich princess'. I had shoved him hard by the beaker shelves and a few jars had crashed to the floor. Mrs. Snapin had gone berserk and screamed at me to be in the principals office the first thing Monday morning, or else.

Or else what?

I knew I was by far the richest fourteen-year-old in the school district. Between my father's inheritance and my mother's old family money, there was nothing they could do to me.

I needed a cigarette.

I tugged at my school uniform's skirt. I hated dresses. I hated the changes my body was going through. I felt deceived. Deceived that time was just moving right along as if nothing had happened.

I picked up some rocks and started hurling them at the trees that lined the way. It felt good to hurt the trees, my brothers. Not a one of them had come to my rescue. I still had night terrors every night. In my dreams I would look up to see my father flying over my head and into the ocean, followed by a stream of women with no faces. And the trees, my tree brothers, would be laughing.

Whack! That was a good one, I thought. The stone had knocked off a small branch before hitting the trunk squarely. That's what you get, that's what you get for laughing!

I stomped into the cottage house, just as the phone was ringing. I knew it was from Principal Nygaurd. My mother barely got the word 'hello' out before I had slammed my bedroom door.

"I see. Yes, yes," my mother said with weariness, "I can come in on Monday. Is that a sister school? You say our local high school is not willing? Yes, I see. Thank you."

I kept my ear pressed to my bedroom door an extra moment, in case my mother had any more to say. But all was quiet, too quiet. Then I heard the clinking of highball glasses being filled with ice. That meant that my mother was going to go to her special place and that I was off the hook until later.

I pulled a pack of Lucky Strikes from under my mattress. I went to my window, opened it, lit the cigarette, and draped myself across the sill on my stomach as I puffed. I had been sneaking smokes for a couple of years and was hooked.

I imagined that my mother would go in on Monday and Principal Nygaurd would say, "That Grace Ruby is such an amazing student, if she would only apply herself." Or maybe he would demand money for the broken beakers. Or maybe he would say that Bill Macken needs to hear an apology.

Well, that was not going to happen. That was never going to happen!

Maybe Principal Nygaurd had a tally sheet of all of my transgressions.

Yes, there had been a few incidents. Well, maybe quite a few incidents that last few years. Did principals keep track of such things?

Well, what did he expect? How many other students' dads had affairs and got caught in the ultimately biggest way possible? How many other kids were snubbed and laughed at every single day because of something that they did not even do?

I flicked the butt to the ground.

Almost four-thirty, I had time before my mother woke up from her alcohol nap.

I slid off the sill and back into my room. I pulled on some capris and my sneakers. What I needed was some ocean air. I needed some open space to fling my anger. The cottage walls were too close. Every day I could feel the walls closing in on me like approaching storm clouds; dark and dangerous. I needed to run and shout to the roaring waves at high tide. "I hate my life, I hate my life!"

Twelve

race tucked little BB into the basket that he had arrived in. She had taken one of her cashmere scarfs and made a little nest in the bottom. He immediately started kneading the soft bedding and snuggled in.

Grace changed out of her Sunday dress clothes and put on some comfortable yoga pants and a Ralph Lauren hoodie. The San Francisco afternoon was gorgeous; crisp and sunny. Grace straightened the kitchen and then grabbed her Prada sunglasses, before taking BB and heading out.

There seemed to be an extra spring in her step as Grace maneuvered the crowded sidewalks of her touristy neighborhood.

Grace was a beautiful woman of sixty-two. She had a thick head of long hair that had turned from blonde to silver. She was tall and slender, and carried herself like a dancer. Today she wore her long, straight hair loose. Every time she crossed a street that ran down to the Bay, an ocean breeze would pick up the strands and lift them off her shoulders.

But there was a little something extra today. Her chin was held higher and her gait a little freer. It all had to do with the precious cargo she was carrying. Grace was feeling the wonderful love pressure of responsibility for something other than herself. Grace was trying something she hadn't done for four decades, and it was invigorating.

"Meow," said BB in a tiny voice when Grace stopped to open the basket lid to check on him.

It's okay, thought Grace as she gave the kitten a scratch under his chin, *almost there.*

~)

The Pet Store was crowded with bird cages and fish tanks. The smell of animal feed accosted her nostrils. Grace found the veterinarian area and headed to the counter. She lifted the basket and placed it by the register.

"We will have to keep him over-night," said the veterinarian nurse. "We'll check his health, inspect for worms, ear mites, give him his first set of shots, and then give him a flea bath."

Grace listened while the nurse rattled on.

"You can pick him up first thing tomorrow morning."

My, what is this feeling I'm having? thought Grace. It seemed to be a new kind of dread. Not a dread of being out of control, but a dread of separation.

Grace lifted the basket's lid and scratched under BB's chin again. He looked up at her with big, fearful eyes.

"I hate leaving him," Grace told the nurse.

"He will be fine. We will take amazing care of him. I'll make sure he is ready to go right at eight when we open."

"Okay," Graced sighed.

Grace shut the lid and headed out into the brisk air. She felt strange; like she had just cut off a piece of her arm and left it on the counter. Intellectually she knew that the vet visit was the right thing to do, it was just that she remembered what it felt like to be sent away as a young girl, and how scary that was.

Can kittens feel abandonment?

Grace said a quick prayer that little BB would know that she would be there to pick him up and give him cuddles. Unlike the day Grace Ruby was left at Lowel Boarding School. No prayers there. None.

Thirteen

Little ghost of white
Sweet laugh under a wide brimmed hat
I see you in my dreams
Dashing through the fern filled woods

You stick out against the darkened trail
Like a pin point of light on shadow
Who could possibly miss your glowing soul
Even through a foggy midnight?

~ ⌒

The fall of 1965, my mother and aunt packed up all of my belongings and had them in the hallway when I came in from one of my ocean runaways. Between my troubles at school and my increasingly disrespectful actions towards my mother, the family had had enough. With the help of Principal Nygaurd, my mother had enrolled me in an exclusive all-girl boarding school in the city.

During the previous summer months, I had been caught shoplifting a tube of mascara and a Payday bar. There was absolutely no reason for me to steal; I had more money than imaginable, but a burning desire to be bad kept floating to the top whenever I had felt anything.

The police had let me go when they realized who I was, but that had just made me angrier.

I had started to wear inappropriate clothing and listening to The Who and the Rolling Stones. I had made friends with kids from the other side of the tracks. I had my first kiss and stayed out late almost every night. I had even taken a risky ride with some older kids to Berkeley to participate in an Anti-War Movement riot.

A friend of my mother had spotted me on a TV news broadcast. That had been the last straw. Behind my back, my mother and aunt had made the arrangements to send me away.

The two women were sitting on my suitcases when I came out of the woods. My face turned as pale as the little girls I had seen one time at the beach, when I realized what was happening.

"No, no, no, I won't go!" I screamed. "Daddy, Daddy, help me Daddy!" I yelled again, as the two older women rushed to block my escape.

Fourteen

Grace put down her pen and looked up at the other diners in the restaurant. Rarely did Grace eat at the many touristy spots that surrounded her, but after dropping BB off back home, she suddenly craved clam chowder.

The walk down Jefferson had been riddled with people. Grace never liked to be in the thick of the crowd, but today had felt different. Her mind was on BB and for some reason that made everything else more tolerable.

The smell of sourdough bread and Ghirardelli chocolate covered the brackish smell of fresh caught sea food; the street artists lured tourists in with their talents; the rattle of cable cars and the distant barking of overweight sea lions at Pier 39...all of it was charming and Grace caught herself smiling.

"Would you like another glass of wine?" asked her waiter.

"Yes please," said Grace, as she dipped the last piece of sourdough into her soup bowl.

"Would you like a little company?" asked another voice from behind her. It was a voice she had never heard, but the tone was deep and rich and sent shivers down her spine. She hoped it was not a fan looking for an autograph. That was the main reason Grace steered clear of popular tourist spots. But when she saw the orange hibiscus coming around her right shoulder she knew... and her whole body reacted with prickles.

Before Grace could even inhale a breath, the tall handsome man that she had silently, often painfully, revered for four decades, graciously pulled out the chair opposite hers and sat down.

~

Five years before, Grace Ruby had started to notice a change in routine for the little family in the house across from hers. Their two children, who were long grown and not living at the house, were coming by more frequently, especially the daughter, who would visit often. In and out of the house she would go, carrying groceries and a long face.

Grace then saw less and less of the wife until about two years ago, when Grace would glimpse the women's handsome husband, drawn and tired, gently steading her down the stairs and into the car.

One day Grace had been on the sidewalk fairly close to the couple and could see the pale palette of sickness replacing the once vibrant women's features. Her handsome neighbor himself was thin and aged with grief.

Then she began to see a series of ambulances, then hospice, and then the last farewell of a reception that follows a funeral, where suddenly folks show up out of the woodwork to offer their condolences. Folks who did not find the time to visit during the painful time of dying, but instead waited to breathe in air cleared of death.

Grace had been sipping tea when she saw the guests on the veranda releasing pink balloons in the fog covered day.

~

And now, here he was sitting directly across from her, the closest she had ever been to this elusive distraction that had honed her powers of reserve.

Grace took a moment. His eyes were gray blue. His once long hair, cut short and flecked with silver. He had a bit of rough stubble along his jaw line. His neck was sun worn and his dress shirt sat perfectly on his frame. But it was his expression that made Grace's spine feel like wobbly gelatin. He was staring at her so intensely that Grace found it hard to draw in a breath. He started to part his lips, to say something, when Grace's paralysis broke.

As fast as she could manage, Grace pushed back from the table and stood up. She reached into her hoodie pocket and threw down a fifty dollar bill. As she turned to flee, she knocked over her glass of wine and stumbled to the door.

Air, fresh air, I can't breathe, thought Grace as she raced down the pier. *This can't be happening? I can't handle all of this: the flowers, the cat, the human connection, the memories; too much has happened in too short of a time.*

Grace was running now, running like she had when she was a girl deep in the bowels of Muir Woods. She let her mind take her back. The cement beneath her feet became redwood bark debris. The strangers she pushed through turned into the giant ferns that would grab at her shoulders. The sky high buildings towered over her like her coastal redwood brothers, tall and protective.

Grace pushed on up the steep city hills, pretending they were her hidden trails leading up from the ocean. Grace's mind went a bit mad, as panic overtook her sensibilities and the elaborate control that she had constructed continued to unravel. She had only one more second of life left when she reached her door. Then she was inside, safe and sound.

Tea, she needed to make tea.

Fifteen

Christmas 1966, I had a year and a few months of boarding school under my belt. My mother had also enrolled me in ballet technical classes.

The advanced dance classes that I attended were grueling. Between my freshman college bound courses and Madame Beauvais' stern regiments of behavior, I had succumbed somewhat to a stringent schedule of rule following.

The first few weeks were unbearable. I had screamed and cried and reverted to foul language when my mother and aunt had dropped me off at Lowel.

The room mothers were brutal and the other girls were just as angry and confused as I was.

There was no forest to run to. The bay water was different then the ocean by my cottage home. There seemed to be no life in the city. The only birds I saw were scavenger gulls hovering over the yard for a neglected snack from a lunch tray. I could not see any ferns or giant redwoods out my bleak dorm window.

The only saving grace to the experience was that there were no boys to tease me and no girls that recognized my wealthy surname.

I began praying. I had not grown up in a religious family, but I knew how to pray. I prayed to be left alone. Then I asked to be rescued. Then I asked if I could disown my family. Then I begged for my father's miraculous return so that he could clear the air. I prayed for my cat's soul. The day that I was dragged away to boarding school, my mother had run over the poor thing. I had been calling for it out the car window. I prayed to wake up from my nightmare.

Sixteen

The Christmas of 1966 was the first time that I was allowed back home and nothing felt normal, nothing at all. I stopped praying when my mother picked me up.

"How could you, how could you?" I kept repeating to my mother as I slammed the front door and stormed off to my room. "How could you just leave me there?"

I flung myself onto my old bed and started crying. So much hurt and confusion was bottled up inside.

The day my father died, I had been broadsided. Just moments before, my entire life had been a fairytale of nature and grace. Each Sidan piece had been carefully played and placed. But then, with just the turn of a wheel, the tower of my childhood had crashed to the rocks by the sea.

My anger was still so raw that I hadn't even noticed how frail my mother looked when she pulled up to take me home for the holiday.

And why was I so angry with my mother, anyway? My mother had absolutely nothing to do with my father's death. Or did she? Perhaps if she had opened her eyes and paid attention, maybe my mother could have noticed his philandering. Maybe if my mother would have been more exciting, or prettier, or..., I had thought.

"Grace, open the door. We need to talk."

I sat up and wiped at my nose with my sleeve.

Yes we do. We most certainly do, I thought as I got up to unlock the door.

Unlike me, who had grown tall and lanky, my mother was petite. She hardly made the bed move when she sat down on its edge. I had backed up to the headboard and pulled my knees up to my chin. I was in a defensive position, ready for battle.

"I am sick," my mother simply stated.

What? What? I screamed in my head. This was not what I expected. This was so not what I expected.

"What?" I asked feebly.

My mother turned her head to gaze out through my bedroom window.

"I have not been well for a long time now, and I'm getting worse," she answered with her eyes avoided.

"What is the matter? Why didn't you tell me?" My voice was stronger now.

"I tried, but you wouldn't listen. You weren't ready to hear."

I gasped in for a breath. I could feel my heart pounding against my legs. Both of us sat frozen, waiting for the other to speak.

"Are you dying?" I finally got out.

"Yes."

My mind immediately began to race.

It's me, it's me. Something about me makes everything die, first daddy, then my kitty, and now this. What's wrong with me?

My mother tried to reach out to me but I retracted and scurried off the bed.

"Everything I love dies!" I shouted.

"That's not true."

"It's because I'm wild and untamed, isn't it? That's what Madame Beauvais says. She says that I have no discipline and that I affect the world negatively. She says that's why you left me there, because I'm dangerous. I'm dangerous, I am!" I was screaming now. I took my arm and flung it across my dresser sending everything crashing to the floor.

I turned towards my mother and saw her slumped shoulders and clasped hands. A feeling washed over me for a moment. What was it, pity, fear, a fading love? Then the feeling was gone and I headed to the front door to escape my feelings with a walk to the ocean.

Seventeen

Christmas near the forest was so different than in the city. No gaudy, too bright lights strung everywhere, just a natural feel; simple and earthy.

December in Muir Woods was typically rainy and drawn in. The coastal redwoods would gather the moisture from a shower and then shelter a person till the storm passed. Then a second rain would occur as the giant trees released the stored water.

The ornaments that hung on these living, outdoor Christmas trees were delicate, small pinecones filled with nuts and stray needles. The huge ferns that shaded the tree's roots would glisten like candy after the second rain. And the smells the winter forest emitted were like living entities themselves... wet and moist...and unforgettable.

I stood under one of my redwood brothers until the quick sprinkle of rain passed. My heart was pounding and heavily in my chest. I still could not wrap my mind around my mother being ill.

Surely she's not dying. Surely there's something that can be done.

I rummaged in my coat pocket for a cigarette. I had tried to quit when I noticed that I had a difficult time keeping up with the other ballerinas in Madame Beauvais' advanced pointe classes, but my addiction had persisted.

Varoom, varoom! Varoom, varoom!

What in the world was that?

54

I pushed the end of my freshly lit cigarette into the wet earth and — stowed it back in my pocket for later.

Varoom!

I climbed back up a small embankment and headed towards the noise. It was coming from the Berkshire's house. Through the thick forest foliage, I could see a burgundy colored muscle car tucked up in the driveway. The hood was raised and the engine was running. Every time the engine roared, a cloud of gray-white exhaust would billow out the tail pipe. The sound was violent in the peaceful setting of the forest, but my whole being began to wake up. The car was incredible. It was gorgeous. It was dangerous. I pushed my hands into my coat pockets and hiked up the drive.

"Hey, hey you there!" I cried out over the noise.

The sound of the engine made me feel brash and brave.

"Hey!" I shouted once again.

The engine cut off and the fading sound reverberated through the tree covered valley. I crossed my arms and waited. After a long moment, a head appeared out from under the hood. I took a step back, as the man/boy walked around the car towards me.

Whoa, I thought. My whole teen girl bravery slid down my spine and spilled onto the driveway. There, standing in front of me, was the hottest guy I had ever seen. He had sandy brown hair with bangs that hung over his eyes. He had on a thick black turtleneck sweater with the sleeves rolled up over his muscular forearms. He was wearing skintight black jeans and Converse sneakers.

I swallowed hard and took a small step back.

"What is it, little girl?" he asked, but he gave away with his eyes that he knew I was not just a 'little girl'.

"What kind of car is making that racket?" I asked. I stuck my chin up in the air and tried to make the tone of my voice more know-it-all.

The boy/man pulled a rag from his back pocket and wiped his hands off slowly, almost seductively. I couldn't take my eyes off of the process.

"Well it's a Pontiac GTO and it has a 335 horse power, 389 cubic inch tri-powered engine with chrome valve covers, and duel exhausts. And it goes zero to sixty in 5.8 seconds." He paused for a moment and I added, "Is that all?"

Then a huge smile bloomed from his face and he started to laugh.

"Way too much car for a little girl like you," he said in between chuckles.

I smiled back at him and said, "Take me for a ride then. Take me out on Highway One. Let's see how fast you both can go."

Eighteen

Men men men
Mighty magnets that
Mesmerize
Mortal women
Making machines
Making memories
Making midnight
Missions of moonlit meetings
Mortal sins full of
Magic and
Madness

~~

Grace Ruby put down her pen when she heard the teakettle whistle. At first she wasn't sure what the sound was. She normally would lift it away before steam pushed though the reeds. She was rattled. *My neighbor showing up during my chowder, was he following me? It seemed he had been following me all weekend.*

Grace picked up her tea and walked the thirteen steps into the front room, or was it fourteen, she suddenly couldn't recall.

Was I really that predictable? Had he secretly been watching out for me all these years? Those little waves from the car, the predictability of his timing, the flowers, the kitten...the face to face meeting!

Grace took a sip and caught her lip on the tiny chip in her favorite teacup.

"Ouch!"

When was the last time that I had been rattled over a man?

Grace knew. She knew it very well.

She put the tea down and got up to rid the view of the orange hibiscus. The bloom was still fresh and full of vibrant color, but Grace plucked it from its vase and threw it in the trash. Then she pulled her heavy front room drapes shut and went to bed.

Eight PM, plenty of time to dredge up an awful dream or two.

Nineteen

I pushed the food around on my plate while sitting across from my mother. In the center of the table was a new table decoration—bottle after bottle of pills lined up like tchotchkes. My mother, or someone, had set up a small Christmas tree and the blinking lights were casting a melancholy feel to the dining room. I took a bite of mashed potatoes and my mother did the same.

"Is it cancer?" I asked quietly.

"Yes, dear."

"Isn't there something that can be done? Have you been to the best doctors?" I asked after we both had taken another bite of potatoes.

"Of course, your grandmother made all of the phone calls and appointments."

"I'll quit school and stay here and take care of you," I said with authority.

"Absolutely not!" answered my mother sternly. Then in a softer voice, "Auntie is going to stay with me and take care of the cottage."

"Maybe they will find a cure. I saw an episode on Ben Casey where they cured a man of lung cancer," I offered.

"Oh yes, maybe," my mother said, as she pushed back from her plate.

"I'm going out later," I said, attempting to change the subject.

"Please don't, please don't get into trouble."

"Just with a friend, just a visit," I lied to my dying mother.

"I can't stop you, can I?" sighed my mother.

I got up and cleared the table while thinking, No, I'm unstoppable!

I pulled on my father's bomber jacket. It was a little big on me, but the faint scent of Old Spice lingered. I lifted the collar to my nose and inhaled.

Midnight was the time mystery boy told me to meet him. I looked at the clock and waited five minutes more; I didn't want to appear too eager.

Out of habit, I crawled out of my bedroom window. I didn't feel like getting into it with my mother. I had been using that escape route for four years now. I knew where every creaky board was and how to avoid it. I had even greased the glides on the window, a couple of years back, so that there would be no squeaks when lifting or lowering.

But just as my feet hit the ground, a flash of bright white caught the corner of my eye. The figure stood completely still for an eerie moment, but then started moving away from me and down the same secret path of my childhood.

I shoved my hands in my dad's coat pockets and followed the ghostly shadow. Who could possibly be out this late, and why are they on my private trail?

When I got closer I saw that the figure was a little girl dressed in a white pea coat. Her hair was the whitest hair I had ever seen. Her tiny head looked like the moon bobbing up and down the path. And in the stillness, I could hear her humming When You Wish Upon a Star.

Soon I came to the fork in the trail that would take me to my rendez-vous. I stopped and watched as the little girl disappeared beneath the ferns and down towards the ocean with the sound of her sweet voice fading away. It almost looked like the forest was swallowing her up, whole.

So odd, she must be doing what I used to do. She's taking a midnight hike to play with the night creatures of the forest, and perhaps dig in the tide-bar sand under the winter stars for little girl treasure.

I pulled a lipstick out of my pocket and rubbed away the innocence of my childhood.

Boys are what I look for now. No time for clams or Sidan games. Hot boys and hot cars, that's the ticket. I said this mantra a few times as I climbed the steep embankment to the waiting muscle car, idling quietly like a purring cat ready to pounce. That's the ticket.

Twenty

K nock, knock, knock.
   What in the world?
Grace was lying face down on the bed with her nose smashed into her pillow. She lifted her head a bit to see the clock.

Knock, knock! Even louder this time.

Twelve midnight.

Who on earth would be calling at this hour?

Even though Grace had lived in and out of the city for six decades, it still sent a shiver and ball of twine into her gut when a knock at the door came unexpectedly. But, it came with the territory, so many wonderful things about living in San Francisco: convenience, artistry, culture, etc., you just had to accept the crime and the crazies along with the amazing.

Grace was always careful. She picked up her billy club from the nightstand, pushed her tangled, long hair out of her eyes and headed toward the peephole.

"Please, open up. It's me, your neighbor."

Grace slowly moved the club into her dominate hand, as she slid her eye into place over the miniscule window.

There he was looking ghostly. The midnight fog had shrouded the city with its floating molecules of moisture. Her porch light sent out a yellow, wet beam of luminosity that made the tall man look unworldly. He shifted from one foot to the next while he waited for her answer.

"I can't let you in. I don't know you," Grace finally got out. She was leaning her whole body against the door.

"But," he answered and then hesitated. "I can't sleep, your drapes are drawn."

Grace pushed into the door even more. Yes, her drapes were closed, just like her heart. She was over sixty years old. She had worked hard keeping life out of her life. Even though she was a famous person, known all over the world, Grace had carefully built a one-woman ark with room for no one but herself. Even the little kitten she was to pick up in the morning could sink the ship. There was no way she could open up to this stranger. In Grace's mind love meant vulnerability, and with vulnerability came endangerment for both parties involved.

Grace turned off the porch light and went back to bed.

Twenty-One

When you wish upon a star...
      Fate
      Love
      Sweet
      Secret

      Bolt
      Fate
      Dreams

～

As I hiked up the last few steps to the car, the boy stepped out with a lit cigarette in his mouth.

"You're late, little girl."

"So?" I said, while lifting my chin.

The night fog was just beginning to creep in from the ocean, like a slow moving breath of silence from the devils den. Both the GTO and the boy were silhouetted against the winter sky.

He had on a black leather jacket, white tee, and jeans, typical look for the times. He looked strong like the male ballerinas that would occasionally be allowed in class to work on lifts with the girls. But this boy was no ballet dancer; there was a wildness about him. He seemed to simmer under a cloak of coolness. I could feel my knees weaken.

"Are you cold?" he asked when he saw that my hands were shoved deep into my pockets.

"Yes," I answered and immediately regretted seeming weak.

"Well get in then."

I hesitated for the briefest of moments. That little nagging feeling of "wake up, this may not be good", came over me. I did not know this boy, really. I knew of the family, but knew nothing of this person. He could be an axe murderer or a kidnapper. He could be one of those men who do terrible things to young, naive girls like me. I looked to the sky for a signal. But all I saw were stars and incoming fog.

"Let's go then!" I yelled a little too loudly in the still December midnight, as I raced around to the passenger's side and pulled the car door (along with my options) shut.

The interior was amazing: deep bucket seats that smelled like new book jackets, round gage windows trimmed in maple veneer and silver metal, an in-dash radio, wood paneling. The boy had the interior light on with the engine running.

"What's your name, little girl?" he asked intimately.

The whole feel of our meeting had changed once we were in the small space.

"Grace Ruby." When he turned his head to look at me, I got a whiff of pomade.

"Grace Ruby, that's a pretty name."

"What's yours, not that I care," I asked with attitude.

He laughed. "You can call me Wally West or Kid Flash, for short!"

"OK Kid Flash, does this piece of junk move or what?"

"Oh it moves alright. You better hold on for dear life, little girl Ruby."

Kid Flash pushed down on the gas while it was still in neutral and revved the engine. I could feel the power and vibrations of the machine earth-quaking from the ground up. Butterflies exploded in my stomach. The last time I had felt this much excitement was when my father had taken me to the Santa Cruz Beach Boardwalk and I had gotten to ride the Giant Dipper rollercoaster for the first time.

Kid Flash killed the internal car lamp, slipped the car in gear, and spun a sharp uey. Gravel kicked back behind the tires and, for a fraction of a second, the car just hovered in place before traction occurred between machine and the earth and the 1966 rocket launched onto Highway One with bursting teen danger fully engaged.

Twenty-Two

Grace put down her pen. She had gotten up early to write more of her memoir. *This is so difficult,* she thought. *Writing this book is like going to therapy.* She recalled the years that her grandmother had dragged her to see Dr. Massy. He would sit there with a pencil behind his ear and ask her all kinds of deep thinking questions. The more he talked, the more Grace had weaved. She had weaved more and more controlled answers. Over and under she would go with fibs and truths, making the basket tighter and tighter until she was locked up snug in protection. It had taken Grace six years to get herself fully sealed up. Her crazy wild emotions had disappeared into the basket's precise, controlled pattern. Grace had slowly and wholly changed her extroversion into introversion and had been able to survive, unscathed for forty-two years.

This morning Grace awoke with one question on her mind: when had she first seen the little white haired girl that haunted her dreams? Over the many years, Grace had never dared tread in the ocean with that one. It was like remembering the snap of a broken bone, or a horribly, embarrassing moment…a person just didn't go searching to relive pain.

This particular morning a memory came to her. In the recollection Grace was probably ten years old and all was well at the cottage. Her father was alive and no one had discovered his indiscretions.

Hadn't she seen a mother sitting on an orange and white checkered blanket spread out on the beach? The woman's hair had been covered in a kerchief and she had a large picnic basket next to her. Grace had noticed her because she was near the spot where Grace liked to dig for clams and it had made Grace irritated.

As Grace walked by to give the woman a 'look', Grace had seen that the woman's attention was straight ahead. Grace had followed her gaze and seen not one, but two little towheaded girls playing in the wet sand!

Grace gasped out loud when this repressed memory flooded her mind. *There were two! Well, this changes things a bit, doesn't it dearie?*

"Yes it does," Grace answered out loud as she grabbed her house key to go down and pick up her new house guest.

Maybe I can find what I have been afraid to search for all of these tormented years…grace, sweet grace.

~⁹

Eight A.M. sharp.

"Meow, meow, meow!" Little BB cried when Grace opened the basket to peek in at him at the pet store.

Oh what sweet bliss is this? Grace thought in rhyme, as she reached in to cup the kitten in her hands. His tiny body vibrated, her palms tingled with happiness. Lifting him to her cheek she listened.

"Purr, purr, purr."

"Thank you for taking him in on a Sunday," Grace called to the same nurse as the night before. Grace took the bill and paid the cashier, then strode out the door.

It was a new day; it was a Monday, a workday for most. San Francisco bustled with a different kind of vibe on work-days. Delivery trucks took over the city; blocking and honking, and thundering up and down the steep streets with squeaky brakes and billows of exhaust.

This spring day was glorious. No wet fog or chilling wind. Grace let her face warm in the sun as she trekked back up to her grandmother's old home, her home. What wonderful things she had learned as a girl staying with her grandmother in moments between pain; her grandmother a perfect balance of strictness and love.

Grace had learned how to be a proper lady from her grandmother. How to eat in a restaurant, what to look for when buying antiques, how to keep an eye on the family's stock portfolio, the proper way to do dishes, how to polish silverware, and most importantly how to structure an intriguing, complete sentence. Grace's grandmother was the one who had discovered and fostered Grace's talent for writing.

Grandmother was also the one who had taken Grace in when her mother had finally passed on.

Grace had been such a mess, so much tragedy in one girl's life. Grace's grandmother had been the best because she had said nothing, nothing about Grace's personality changes. She had just let her be. Grace had just let her grandmother wind her protective cocoon around her life.

She and her grandmother had mourned together in the safety of their home, a home set deep in the concrete forest of San Francisco. And while they had mourned, Grace had slowly metamorphosed into a gifted, introverted writer.

~9

Eight-forty A.M., home. Grace opened the basket, lifted little BB out, and placed him on the floor. For a moment the kitty was disoriented, then he saw his little food bowl and all was well. Grace couldn't take her eyes off the little living creature in her kitchen. The whole room seemed brighter with him in it.

Did her neighbor somehow know that she needed a breath of life? Had he been watching her as much as she had been watching him all of these years? Was it fate the times that they would pass by each other? Could he somehow sense that she was experiencing a death of her own, the death of a secret?

Grace tucked little BB back in the towel resting at the foot of her bed and headed into the den to write.

She made a whispered vow to open the front room drapes if she made it through the next few pages. It would be a dramatic gesture. She would grab the sashes at four or a little after, and then wrench them open to let some glorious, neighborly light inside!

Grace took a breath and put her pen to paper.

Twenty-Three

I was finding it hard to breathe. The GTO was tearing around each hairpin corner barely gripping the road. Kid Flash appeared to use every fiber of muscle in his forearms to hold the wheel in place as he accelerated through each turn. The straightaways felt like a drag race. The boy never touched the brakes.

Inside the car we both were screaming and hollering with crazed joy. I had one hand on the dash and the other holding tight to the door grip. Just when I would relax a bit, the car would veer towards the wrong side of the road and a steep cliff leading down to the ocean.

"AAAH!" I would scream and Kid Flash would yank the car back into the correct lane and we would both laugh hysterically.

"Hold on, little girl Ruby," he yelled as he floored the accelerator. "Hold on!"

The car finally slowed as we headed into Stinson Beach. My whole body was quivering like gelatin. I looked down and could see my chest heaving in and out as my heart tried to pump blood back into my pale cheeks.

"That was amazing!" I shrieked with exhilaration. "Your car is amazing!"

Kid Flash pulled the GTO into the parking lot at the Sand Dollar.

"How about a soda pop?" he asked.

I was out the door before he could finish. I walked over and waited for him to lock the doors. Then I put my arm in the crook of his.

We walked up to the diner and went in. We found a window seat and sat side by side. Kid Flash ordered two colas and a basket of fried clams with ketchup.

"I want to drive it," I stated matter of factly, after we had devoured half of the order.

"What? No way. That's way too much car for little girl Ruby."

"I can do it, I know how to drive," I lied.

"How old are you?" he asked.

Again I lied, "Seventeen."

"Okay, maybe. For a kiss?" he said as he paid the bill.

"Alright, one kiss, but you better make it a good one," I teased as we headed for the car.

~

Kid Flash drove the GTO slowly down Calle del Mar Road to Look Out Point and parked. The ominous fog bank was creeping ever closer. We both sat uncomfortably in the silence staring not at the view, but at our inner thoughts.

"Gum?" offered the boy.

"Sure." I loved Black Jack.

I chewed quickly to get the full black licorice flavor and to mask my cigarette breath. Kid Flash did the same.

"How about that kiss?" the boy asked and I could feel my body liquefying.

I had experienced a few kisses in my fourteen years; quick, sloppy kisses from boys my own age. Boys that didn't have a clue what they were doing. But I knew this kiss was going to be different. This would be a very grown up type of kiss. I partially closed my eyes and leaned across my bucket seat and waited.

Kid Flash hesitated and smiled for a moment perhaps at the sweetness of my anticipatory expression, and then he took both of his hands and cupped my face, pulling my lips onto his.

My mind fired up. I didn't want to miss one second of the experience. I cracked open my eyes even wider and saw that his were shut. There was a springy feel to his plump lips. When he interlocked his fingers behind my head and neck and pulled me even closer, a fire lit up in my belly. This was no 'behind the dugout' kiss. There was no spit or horrible tongue. This was a passionate true first kiss, deserving of a lasting memory of a life-time.

I pulled away and inhaled a quick breath.

"Now change seats with me. My turn to drive," I piped up, completely changing the mood. "I'll drive around this parking lot to get the feel, and then I will take you home."

"Take ME home? Oh little girl Ruby, you are too much," the boy said, as he got out of the driver's side with no sense of dread or flash of regret.

And the fog began to roll in from the sea, mimicking our breath steaming the windshield.

Twenty-Four

Little white lies we tell
To protect our fragile egos
Sometimes turn bloody red
And become devouring monsters
That eat at our fragile souls
Until we are no longer
Who we were
But who we
Aren't

~

I put both hands on the wheel and then reached down and turned the key. My nerves were like live, cut wires. The lies about my age and my driving ability were burning an edgy hole in my gut.

I took a breath and pushed on the gas with my en pointe right foot. I imagined rising up on my toes with the releve method, where the dancer rises smoothly by rotating the foot downward until it is fully extended. The car answered by roaring. I then pulled down on the gear shift, and the car lurched forward.

"Yikes! Easy now, little girl Ruby," Kid Flash said with a laugh. "You sure you know how to drive?"

I moved my right foot to the brakes and pushed down hard. We both jerked forward and then laughed.

"Hold on, just give me a second," I said, as I tried everything for a second time.

Soon I was maneuvering the car smoothly around the empty parking lot.

"Well let's roll," Kid Flash said, as he lit a cigarette and let me have a drag.

The GTO seemed to sense its delicate driver and stayed subdued as I turned onto the empty highway and headed back towards Muir Woods.

Driving is a piece of cake, I thought, as I eased the car faster.

Kid Flash turned on the radio and Wild Thing by the Troggs came blasting out.

Piece of cake, I thought once more as I bobbed my head to the music.

"Want a swig?" the boy offered as he pulled a bottle of Pear Ripple out of the glove box.

"Ah, no thanks," I yelled over the music.

One thing that I didn't like was alcohol. It reminded me of the days following my father's death and the way my mother dove into the bottle. Plus, I was really trying to hold it together as I started up the windy road.

"Suit yourself," said Kid Flash. He tipped the bottle up and chugged away.

My mind began to wander as the fog's tendrils started to crawl up the steep cliffs of Highway One. I kept seeing the little girl in white in my mind's eye. It almost seemed like a mirage now; a mirage of myself, as a little girl. Perhaps my mind was just playing tricks on me. Was the vision just an apparition of myself as a child?

I had been such a happy, outgoing little girl with no cares and no fears. I had loved living beside my dense forest playground. And now, as a teenager, I was forced into a school of concrete living with the real possibility that I would soon be an orphan. If I was to see a ghost of what I looked like now, that figure would be as black as tar. No glowing aura of sweetness; that apparition would be full of bitter anger and building rage.

I started pushing down on the gas pedal harder. The powerful GTO responded by thundering up and down the steep hills.

"Faster, faster," Kid Flash yelled as I got more and more daring.

The boy took another swig from the bottle as Paperback Writer came on the radio.

Both of us began to sing the chorus, "Paperback writer, paperback writer!"

I knew what I was doing was illegal. I knew that I had deceived the boy. I didn't want to get caught by the police driving underage. But in the moment, none of that mattered. I just felt wild, alive and dangerous. That excitement numbed my past and revved up my future. Paperback writer, oh yeah!

I maneuvered the car around the hairpin turns, but as I entered a short straightaway, the fog reared its shrouded head.

"Go, go, go Grace Ruby!" the boy shouted. "Show no fear!"

I slammed down on the gas pedal and the muscle car shot forward like a bullet.

Immediately, a figure of white was before us. A flash of eyes reflected. I plowed through the creature as it hit the front bumper and then smashed across the windshield. The GTO began to skid sideways. I overcorrected and then the car rolled.

That strange phenomenon of time moving in slow motion occurred while I was screaming. The boy was tumbling around in the front part of the car. He looked like a gold-fish in a bowl going round and round. I saw his head crack on the windshield. Somehow I held on to his body and it acted like a shield as we twisted and turned. At one point I felt my ankle snap and knew in an instant that my ballet days were over.

But it was the sounds that made everything a million times worse, the thud and then the crack. The boom of the car tipping onto its side. The loud screeching of metal on pavement, glass breaking. The radio, turned up to its maximum volume, blared through the impact and beyond.

"What did I hit, what did I hit?" I screamed. "A deer, please be a deer!"

That flash of white seems all too familiar, I thought right before I lost consciousness.

～

I came to a few minutes later. I could feel the car still settling. At first I thought I had fallen asleep at the Sidan table with my father. My head was lying across something hard and the radio was blaring Play With Fire, by the Stones.

Whose turn is it Daddy? I said in my mind.

Then the horrifying realization of my situation crept in like winter fog the head over the highway.

I opened my eyes a crack and saw that I was staring at the car's radio. The dash lights were on and the music was deafening. I reached my hand out and turned it off. The silence was even louder.

I licked my lips and they tasted salty and metallic. I was afraid to move. I tried speaking.

"Hey, hey are you okay?" Somehow I knew that he wasn't. I called his name louder. "Kid Flash, say something!" Nothing. No answer.

I rocked my head back and forth gingerly, to feel what I was lying on. It felt like a hip. It was. My head was on the boy's hip. It was so strange being this intimate; like we were cuddling in some strange position. I tipped my head up a bit and had vertigo. The car had come to rest on its left side and somehow through the rollover the boy had ended back in the driver's seat. I turned my head to the right and could see the passenger's side bucket seat high up in the air, with the entire right side dash pushed up to the leather.

What's that smell? It was a mix of excrement and pears.

I used the boy's side to lift up against gravity. Pieces of glass slid down the back of my neck. The headlamps were still on, but the fog was so thick that the light couldn't escape and instead reflected back into the car.

I screamed when I tried to move my right leg from its resting place over the gear shift box. My left leg was tucked under me like I was sitting on the couch watching Ed Sullivan.

"Help, help," I said feebly and started to cry.

What have I done? I let my mind go into pity mode. I've let myself get totally out of control. Now I've had an accident and I've hurt others. What was I trying to do anyway? What was I trying to prove? Did I think that I was invincible? Was I trying to say to the world, 'I don't care what you think of me or my family; I don't care what you say?' Was I trying to kill myself?

I started sobbing as I let those thoughts race through my mind.

Then I felt him move beneath me.

"Hey, hey, wake up!"

I reached up and rubbed the boy's arm and chest. A horrible strange sound gurgled out of him. I rubbed his belly with my right hand and pushed up with my left without moving my leg.

Oh his face, his beautiful face!

I screamed again and passed out.

In my dream I was chasing a fawn through the forest. I was little, maybe ten. The fawn was as white as snow; a rare albino fawn. Every time I would get close to her, the baby deer would scamper off.

I looked down and saw that I was carrying my old orange bucket. Inside the bucket were Sidan pieces. I kept dropping puzzle pieces so that I wouldn't lose my way.

Finally I chased the fawn to the edge of a cliff and watched it sail down to the ocean below to its death.

I put the empty bucket on my head and then heard voices in the distance.

"Look, look, there are two kids in here!" It was a man's voice. I squinted as a flashlight shined in my face, waking me from my dream.

"Call it in. Call for an ambulance. Oh my God, look at this car!" This was a different voice.

My mind raced out of control. I knew that I was the one driving and that I had hit something that was in the road. But I was just fourteen, not seventeen like I had told Kid Flash. I was sure that I would go to jail.

What to do, what to do?

"Look, at the passenger's side. The whole front end is pushed up to the dash," said voice number one.

"The trees, they landed in the trees," said number two. "The trees saved their lives, if they are alive. Look how close to the cliff they are!"

My stomach started to heave. Oh no, I'm going to throw up.

"Help, help," I said feebly.

"Hey, one's alive! Hold on honey, hold on!"

By now the blanket of gray was subsiding. Nothing was going to be able to be hidden. Through a giant crack in the windshield I could see a few stars in the winter sky. I thought of the song the little ghost was singing, about wishing on stars.

Was fate going to see her through?

I tried to rouse the boy again. Nothing. Then a lie came to me. It came as clear as a sunny day on my cottage porch.

I twisted my head to see if I could see it. Ah yes, there it is. The bottle of Ripple had survived the crash. I could see that it was lodged under the gas pedal. How convenient? My on the spot story was coming along nicely.

Then there came a bloodcurdling scream. It was the worst kind because it came from a grown man. The sound of it echoed through the shattered windshield and across the still forest.

"What is it, what is it?" called one of the men.

"Oh my God, oh my God!"

"What?"

"It's a little girl and her head is cut off!"

I threw up and then blacked out once again.

Twenty-Five

Liar, liar pants on fire
Hangin' on a telephone wire
Moved my lips
Sunk a ship
And lost my soul in a doughnut fryer

~⁀

Grace put down her pen; she was crying. Big round globes of salty ocean drops were pouring out of her tear ducts. There it was. There it was for all to see, her horrible, wretched lie out in the open.

"Meow." Grace reached down and picked up little BB. She sat him on her writing desk and wiped at her tears with the back of her hand.

"I'm a horrible, horrible person," Grace said to the kitten.

BB batted at Grace's pen and then flopped down on his side on top of her notebook.

"Purr, purr, purr," the kitten offered.

Grace picked up her pen again with shaky fingers.

When the police came to me in the hospital, I set my lies in motion.
I told them that the boy I was with had been drinking and driving and

that he had totaled the car. I said that it had been foggy and that he had hit a deer.

The two policemen at the foot of my hospital bed stopped questioning me for a moment and turned and looked at each other.

"What about my boyfriend? What about Kid Flash?" I assumed he was dead.

"Now don't you worry about him," said the older policeman. "He's alive, but in a coma."

What, what? I immediately had two conflicting reactions. The first was, Thank God he is alive! And the second was, Oh my God, he's alive. What if he tells the truth?

I almost let my reaction out, but quickly reeled it back in. If my lie is to work, then I'm going to have to be careful of what I say, what I do…everything.

My stomach knotted up into a tangle of fishing worms. That's what lying feels like. I did not want my mother to know that I had gone out at midnight with an older boy. I didn't want her to know that he was a stranger. I didn't want the police to know that I had manipulated the boy into letting me drive, for a kiss. I didn't want the world to know that I had murdered someone, a little girl, a little innocent girl who was just like me at one time!

I pulled the first cane of my deceitful basket through my life and began weaving my many fibs, one after another while sitting in the hospital waiting to hear if Kid Flash had recovered, or not.

The last day I was in the hospital, I asked my nurse to wheel me over to see Kid Flash. I had found out his real name was Mike Berkshire. He was the oldest of three boys that had grown up not too far from our cottage.

Mike's parents stayed at the hospital day and night, waiting for their son to wake up. He had wires sticking out of his arms and his head was completely covered with bandages.

As my nurse wheeled me in, his parents apologized for their son's actions. I lied with a nod of my head and held in my guilt tears.

"They say he will never be the same, that he is a vegetable now," sobbed Mrs. Berkshire.

"Now, now dear, we mustn't give up hope," added Mr. Berkshire.

"And that poor baby, what was she doing out that late in the middle of the road?" Mike's mother wailed as her husband tried to console her. He put his arm around her and led her out into the hallway.

My nurse wheeled me up to the boy's bed and left.

"My first real kiss. My last taste of wild abandon. My first crush. I will never be untamed again. I promise to be careful and precise. I promise to not love or be loved ever again. I promise to never hurt another soul!"

I held the boy's hand as I recited my prayer in a whisper. I let my free, feral spirit die in that instant. My days of running loose in the woods were over. No more ballet or thoughts of driving. No school dances or midnight escapes. Every remaining day of my life would be spent in controlled penance for my sins. My lies would keep me from experiencing joy. I put myself in my own prison and then threw away the key.

Part Two

Twenty-Six

Two-thirty P.M., just enough time to get everything done. Grace got up and blew her nose on a tissue. BB was sound asleep on her bed, curled up in his towel.

I hope I have some? She thought to herself as she headed to the hall closet.

Then she went back to her writing den and made a copy of each page from chapters twenty-one through twenty-five. She drummed her fingers impatiently while the copier droned.

A box, I need a box as well. Grace thought for a moment then went to retrieve the box BB's food and water bowls had come in. *This will do.*

Grace took the pages and placed them carefully into the cardboard box. She layered a few pieces of tissue paper and then sealed the box with tape. She cut off some orange wrapping paper and covered the box; neatly folding and creasing each tuck.

Hurry, hurry, she said to herself. Grace did not want to lose her nerve.

Now what? Oh yes, a note. I must attach a note.

After tying the same ribbon that had been on BB's basket securely around the orange package, Grace attached a scented note card and simply wrote:

My hair is down...
Rapunzel

Two forty-five P.M., "I need to hurry," Grace said out loud to her sleeping kitten.

Grace pulled on a sweater and headed down her steep outdoor steps. The fog was just starting to roll over the pier. She walked quickly with the package held out in front of her as if it was a tea service. No one took notice; she just looked like another San Francisco loon.

For the very first time ever, Grace Ruby walked through to the narrow entrance way to her neighbor's. The staircase leading to his front door was made of wrought iron. The door itself was made from coastal redwood. Grace paused and pressed her face into the wood and inhaled. Memories of her brothers of Muir Woods flooded her senses.

"What am I doing?" she whispered to the solid door before her.

Grace inhaled another quick breath and then placed the orange 'bucket' of confession on his welcome mat, and scurried back across the busy street.

〜〤

Three P.M., *Phew, I made it,* Grace thought as she lifted the teakettle off the stove and poured the hot water over her teabag. She placed her favorite cup on its saucer and walked into the living room. This time her gait was unsteady and some of the tea spilled over onto the saucer.

Before she sat down, she looked at her tête-a-tête settee. How ironic that piece of furniture was. Here it was before her representing so much: the yin and the yang, the before and the after, the truth and deceit, extrovertism and introvertism, childhood and adulthood, together and alone, penalty and grace, and most importantly, duality.

Grace sat down before her closed drapery covered window. BB sat at her feet and chewed on her shoelace.

Today is a pivotal day for me. Good or bad, right or wrong, I have set something in motion.

"Tick tock," said her grandfather clock. Grace sipped her tea and noticed that she had forgotten to add the canned milk and honey.

My routine is unraveling.

"Tick tock." Finally, at one minute before four, Grace sat her tea down and went over to the big picture window that faced the north. With crazed dramatic flair, Grace Ruby hauled down on the drapery pulls and yanked the heavy curtains open just as the clock chimed four.

BB skirted under the settee to hide. He had never seen his human move so fast. Looking down onto the street Grace saw that she had missed him; his car was already in its place.

Oh well, it's done.

"Here BB, here BB," Grace called as she squatted down on the floor.

The kitten didn't seem to know what to do. He hadn't really heard his name yet.

"Here kitty, here BB."

When he saw that she had calmed down he came out from under the chair and ran to her with his little kitty tail sticking straight up in the air.

Grace's heart moved a little in her chest.

Was that love? she thought. It had been so, so long since she had felt that feeling. She picked up her baby and nuzzled him to her neck.

Five past four. *What would her neighbor think? That was the question, wasn't it?*

Grace put little BB on the attached seat of the settee and pulled out the opera glasses, typical late afternoon Monday in the city; tourists and locals intermingling without mixing. Grace put her attention everywhere except her neighbor's home.

Four forty-five. "Tick tock." *Nothing.*

Grace drained the remaining swallow of tea.

How long does it take to read a few confessional chapters? Maybe he didn't even notice the box, or maybe someone took it. Maybe he can't find his reading glasses, or maybe he doesn't like the written word and prefers electronic. Or...and this was the fear, maybe he has read it and is so shocked and appalled that he will now forever be repulsed by the thought of me.

Grace got up quickly and went into the kitchen.

I need air. I need to think. She put some food out for BB, picked up her writing things, and headed down to the bay.

The spring fog had stopped short of coming on shore. The setting sun was the only thing disappearing into darkness. She walked down to the Black Point Café as the street lights began popping on like fireflies.

She ordered a turkey and avocado on sourdough, and suppressed her claustrophobic feelings at the crowded window area. She closed her eyes and let her mind take her back to Muir Woods at the ocean's edge. She inhaled the woodsy scent and felt the crumbled bark beneath her feet. She found a rock and sat Indian style, in her mind, in a small patch of sun. She transported herself back in time, a time where she was a good girl and she hadn't bitten the devil's apple.

Grace opened her eyes and began to write.

I had wanted to be a Sherpa when I was ten—a Tibetan tribal member that leads trekkers up and down the Himalayan Mountains. I had read about them in one of my father's National Geographic magazines. I knew that I could do it because I was exceptional at hiking up and down the steep cliff areas of the Pacific Ocean coast. The job would be perfect for me (at age ten) because I would be completely outdoors with no walls to confine my soul. I would meet interesting people and get to work with animals. There would be no schoolwork or housework, just beautiful vistas and nature all around.

That is not how my dream went. Events happened. Avalanches of trouble had poured down, with boulders of pain to stumble over and icy feelings to conceal. Oh I had met interesting people, but I had made no emotional connections. I had confined my vistas to those I could view out of the safety of my bay window. My whole life's direction had veered off track the day my father had sailed overhead during one of nature's downpours.

Instead of correcting myself, I had let my undeveloped ego take charge. I had gotten on top of the 'guilt' animal and ridden it to the next tragedy shouting, "Poor me, poor me!" I had become more and more bitter with each negative event. I had attracted unhappiness. Then I toyed with cool. Teenage cool is the devils game. It's an age that dissolves all sense of danger and fear. This is when I had gotten on the bucking bronco and risked my life to end my pain. But instead of just hurting myself, I had taken the lives of others.

~

Grace slid off the rock in her mind and opened her eyes in the busy coffee shop on Larkin. She was exhausted—exhausted from running. She needed to tell the truth. That was why she had opened up to her neighbor. A baby step to release. Her shoulders were worn down from hiding her true self. She wasn't looking for forgiveness or pardon; she just needed to dig herself out from under the mountain of deceitful rubble that had fallen on her living coffin. She just needed help moving just one stone— just one pebble. She needed a Sherpa to lead her up the mountain.

~

It was late when Grace Ruby trekked up her steep street. Walking was always therapy. Her fractured ankle had long ago healed after the accident. The hills of San Francisco had acted as physical rehabilitation. Grace did her best thinking while walking. When she was stuck with writer's block she walked. When Lord Byron couldn't figure out a clue she walked. When the pressures of being a famous author piled on top of her, she walked.

Now her walking mind floated to her handsome neighbor. She pictured the orange wrapped box in his hands. He had such beautiful eyes. Her up-close view of him was so much better than she could have imagined. She was so rude in the restaurant. *Why did I leap from the table without even so much as an apology? I didn't even ask his name.*

And is it just some divine coincidence that he is reaching out to me while I write pivotal moments in my memoir? Has he been watching me recently? Has he kept an eye on me over the years, even when his beautiful family was alive and flourishing? Is he being offered to me by a power that I have searched for every Sunday?

How many love affairs are postponed until later in life? When circumstances change, or traumatic events resolve. How many folks find love in the senior years of their lives, true love, love that is not dependent on the past?

Grace's mind was racing as she climbed the steps to her front door.

Twenty-Seven

Keys open, close, unlock, reveal
Keys type, make music, or dial
Keys explain symbols on maps and tables
Keys provide a set of answers to problems
Keys solve codes
Keys are things that provide a means of understanding
Keys open, close, unlock, reveal

What's this? Grace thought. Hanging from her front door handle was a key on a piece of orange ribbon. *Is that the same ribbon that we have been passing back and forth?*

Grace looked back over her shoulder and down to the street below. No one was there.

She lifted the strand off the door and put it around her neck like a necklace. It surprisingly had weight, both figuratively and literally.

BB was waiting inside and sat on his backside looking up at her when she came in. When she picked him up he batted at the key and chewed on the ribbon.

What did this mean? Why did he give me a key, and a key to what?

Grace walked into the front room and stood in front of her picture window bravely.

San Francisco at night is something to behold, the density of light looks like an earthbound meteor shower.

Grace inhaled and looked down across the street at her neighbor's house. There was a light on. A dim light, compared to the rest of the city.

Can he see me? Grace stepped closer to the pane and opened her arms in a gesture of surrender. Nothing. And then...a quick flick. *Did that just happen?*

Grace backed up, knocking over a Lladro figurine of St. Teresa writing with a dove that Carla, her agent had given her when Grace had sold her third book.

Crash! BB scurried out of the room and into the kitchen.

Oh dear, this man has me so rattled! Grace thought as she bent down to retrieve the pieces.

"Why a key?" she said out loud to BB. "What does that...?"

Grace suddenly had an idea. She stumbled into her writing room and looked at the last sentence of the pages that she had offered to him. It said:

"Grace put herself in her own prison and then threw away the key."

Grace lowered her notebook slowly to the table. *This man has been speaking to me in symbols and gestures, keying me in to what is on his heart. Years of little waves, orange hibiscus flowers, orange kitten, a key on an orange ribbon! In my quest to keep my vow of unconnectedness, have I inadvertently hurt someone anyway?*

Grace pulled at the strand around her neck and fiddled with the key. She had never imagined that her aloofness and introvertedness would hurt someone. She had only imagined that her involvement with anyone would somehow cause them harm. That is the premise she had been living with all these years. But what if she was wrong? What if while she was busy being alone, others in the world missed out on her? Did she have something to offer besides made-up, who-done-it mysteries? Could she have been a wife or even a mother?

Electrical charges started firing up in Grace's belly. Her breathing quickened. Goosebumps formed on the backs of her forearms.

What time is it, anyway?

Nine-thirty, is that too late?

Grace decided, at that very instant, that she would do something that she hadn't done since she was a girl—head out into the night with no plan… no plan what so ever.

~~

Knock knock. Grace stood shaking in front of her neighbor's front door. No answer. She tried again.

Knock knock, *this is crazy. This is so wild and uncharacteristic of adult me. Here I am knocking on the door of a virtual stranger like a love struck teen.*

Grace then looked down at the key hanging around her neck.

Do I dare? It does look like a house key. What's the worst thing that could happen? That it doesn't fit? That I look like a fool?

Grace lifted the ribbon over her head and pushed the key into the lock. At first it wouldn't go in. The key seemed uncomfortable and rusty, like her. Then, with a slight turn of the wrist, the key slipped into the slot and the door unlatched.

"Hello," Grace offered quietly as she opened the door.

"Come in Rapunzel," said a man's deep voice.

Grace stepped in and was amazed.

The whole entry was filled with orange hibiscus plants. It looked like a florist's showroom. The lights were dimmed and theatrical. There were floor spots and cans of track lighting pointed at the foliage.

Grace took a big breath in and just looked around. The deco style home had been modernized with the look of a loft. Beyond the entry was a huge space filled with greenery and oversized furniture. The life in the home was so different than the dried up potted plants on his veranda that Grace could see from her living room window. She felt like she had just stepped outdoors, rather than in.

"Are you going to run away from me again?" he asked.

As Grace's eyes adjusted she could see him sitting in a large leather chair with his legs crossed. She had no idea what to say.

"Please, come sit down," he offered, indicating the couch next to him.

Grace felt like a forest deer edging her way closer to something dangerous. She sensed that in the next few moments, her life was going to change forever. She sat down on the end of the couch farthest away from him.

"I'm sorry about the loss of your wife," she spoke. Her voice was soft and a bit raspy from under use.

"Me too. The thief, cancer," he replied.

Grace's heart was pounding; her spine felt uncomfortable.

She could feel his eyes on her as he waited for her to speak.

"I lost my mother to the same thief."

After a pause, "Yes, I know."

Grace's mind raced. *How did he know that? Did I put that in a bio at some point?* Then she remembered the pages she had given him.

"Wine?" he offered.

"Yes," she answered way too quickly.

He got up and Grace followed him to the kitchen area.

The space was beautiful, dark red stained cabinets, counters covered with distressed tin, thin multi-colored glass lights hanging across the bar. Nothing like she had imagined.

"Red or white?" he asked while his back was turned from her.

"White, please."

He handed her the glass but didn't release the stem for a fraction of a second. Grace's stomach loosened.

"A toast?" he asked.

"To what?" Grace raised her glass to his.

"Yesterday was my last day of work. I am officially retired."

Grace broke out into a smile, a big genuine smile of relief. This was so not what she expected him to say. She let her shoulders drop and relaxed a bit. She touched her glass to his.

"Congratulations!"

"Yes, I was ready. I just turned sixty-six and I'm ready for a new adventure. How about a snack?"

As he talked, he unbuttoned his shirt at the cuffs and rolled up both sleeves. Grace couldn't help but stare at his muscular forearms as he sliced some cheese and rinsed green grapes in the sink.

Grace took a big sip of wine and said, "I will probably never retire."

"Well, that's because you are doing what you love, what you were meant to do."

He knows that I'm an author. That's obvious.

He put the plate of goodies in front of her and popped a grape into his mouth.

Grace thought about his words. In one sense he was right, but in another he had missed the mark. She really wrote fantasy to avoid reality.

"Something like that, I suppose," she answered.

"Come on, let's go back and sit down."

Grace picked up her glass and wandered around the living room a bit. The high walls were a muted silver gray, and were covered in giant abstract paintings. Purples and emerald greens, with burgundy and white accents. All bordered with thick black frames.

"Who's the artist?" Grace asked without turning her head away from the art.

"I am," he answered modestly.

"They're fantastic! For some reason, they remind me of the woods where I grew up."

"Just a distraction, a hobby," he offered offhandedly.

Grace moved to an alcove. Framed photos were hung in a checkerboard pattern— alternating colored with black and whites. Here were the visual imprints of his family frozen in time. Grace recognized all of the faces—his wife, children, even him over the years. *How sweet his daughter's face is with birthday cake on it? And here's his son in his high school baseball uniform. Oh, and I recognize that little pink coat the girl is wearing. She wore that for years.* But as Grace's eyes wandered across the pictorial history before her, tears started pooling. His wife, his partner...she was so present at that time. In every shot, she looked so alive, so out going.

What am I doing? Grace suddenly felt claustrophobic in the huge house. It seemed big and empty, but it wasn't, it was filled with memories and laughter and family.

"I'm sorry, but I must be going," Grace said while heading for the door.

"What? No wait. We need to talk. I need to talk to you about something, about what you wrote!" He was trailing after her now, reaching for her arm.

"No, no. Not now. I can't."

"Just this, just this then," he said and as she got to the door he pulled at her arm and drew her into an embrace.

She resisted and he pulled her in tighter and held her completely against his body.

"Just breathe little girl, just breathe," he whispered.

Grace's heart leapt into her throat as she pushed him away and stumbled out the front door.

"I don't even know your name. What's your name?" she got out between sobs.

"Michael," she heard him say as she rushed out to the street below. "It's Michael."

$\sim$

*B*ang! Grace slammed the door, ran into her bedroom, and flung herself on her bed.

What just happened? Did I hear him correctly? Did he call me 'little girl'? Were those exact words in the chapters that I gave him? Was this stranger playing tricks on me?

Grace sobbed out loud and let her mind go over the events that just happened.

Everything was going along nicely, until I grasped I was in another woman's home. I actually had forgotten about my confession for a moment, and was focusing on the ramifications of having a possible relationship with a widower.

But then, those forearms, those paintings, his tone of voice. His name!

Grace could hardly let her mind go there. *Could he possibly be the boy in the GTO? My first real kiss? My silent partner in crime? And living across from me all these years? What kind of deception is that?*

BB risked coming over to his human when he saw that she was in pain. He put on his cutest expression and crawled over to her splayed hair to make a kitty bed.

Grace reached up and scratched his head.

The last thing she remembered was the boy's mother saying that he would be a vegetable or possibly never wake up at all. *Could the doctors have been wrong? And why wasn't I ever told?*

All these years of believing that she had taken him from his mother; was it possible that this neighbor, her neighbor was this same boy? But he didn't look familiar at all. He was around the same height and build, but his face was not the one that she remembered. *Maybe this is a scam. Maybe this guy is a crook and everything is a lie. Maybe he is just after my money?*

Grace got up and BB tumbled onto the pillow. It was late. She needed to sleep so that she could think clearer in the morning.

She washed her face and brushed her teeth. And fell immediately into a horror filled dream.

Twenty-Eight

Always changing always evolving
With the same constant elements
A rock is not the same rock it woke up to be
A million years before
Egg caterpillar cocoon butterfly
Seed root stem leaf bloom
Ova baby child teen adult
Shy quiet curious brave loud wild wise
Metamorphosis is what propels the universe
To return again and again to the
Eternal truths

~~

In Grace's dream she was sitting alone on Muir Beach. Her orange clam bucket was beside her and she was busy digging for clams. This time Grace was not a little girl, she was sixty-two years old. Her long silver hair was being blown back by the gentle winds coming off the Pacific Ocean. Overhead the sun was bright and the sky was a beautiful blue. Grace was looking down and concentrating on her task.

After a while, Grace felt a presence behind her. It was Madame Beauvais, her strict ballet teacher. As the old woman approached,

Grace saw that she had something in her arms. It looked like a large block of wood. In a flash, the woman was beside her and placed the block on the sand next to Grace and then disappeared.

Hmmm, that is odd. Grace kept digging.

Then she heard a gull cry and looked up to see Lord Byron, her protagonist from her novels. He looked dashing in his ascot and navy trench coat.

"Keep digging, dear author, keep digging" he shouted to her, as he too, placed a wooden block on the sand next to Grace then vanished.

"Scavare per vongole Grace Ruby?" Giovanni asked. "Digging for clams?"

"Why yes," answered Grace, while she watched her favorite restaurateur place his block in front of her with added flair.

Ethel Vogelzang and Carla Lingam materialized and added their blocks on top of the others.

Grace could see that they were building a little fortress around her. She didn't feel worried; in fact it made her feel safe.

She began to hum.

Then a cloud passed in front of the sun and the sand turned dark.

Grace looked up and saw her mother and father standing on the other side of her barricade. They had long sad faces and moved in slow motion. Grace felt angry and fearful as she watched them set their blocks on top, forming another layer. She tried to cry out to them, but no sound came out. Their images dissolved like smoke into the thin ocean air.

Grace started humming again. *When You Wish Upon a Star* was the tune.

Then the deliveries came faster.

Drunk Auntie Mae, Bill Macken the bully from grammar school, even Dr. Massy, Grace's psychiatrist...each of them carried two blocks and piled board on top of board. Grace was starting to panic. She hummed even louder. Her Sidan tower was going up higher and higher. The louder she hummed the faster it went up.

The sky dimmed above her with evil fog. Grace could hear voices outside her towering tomb. The walls were well above her head and the fog dropped down like a misty lid.

Grace screamed, "Help, help!"

Nothing.

Then she heard it.

Varoom, varoom!

Grace bent down and peered out between the spaces in the puzzle pieces. And there it was!

Varoom, varoom, errkkk!

The burgundy GTO was barreling across the sand straight for her fortress; the fortress that she now was trapped in.

Who is that driving? That was her only thought as the car rammed into....

~9

Grace bolted straight up in bed with the image of a face shattering the barrier between dreaming and waking. Her heart was pounding as she recalled the nightmare. In it she was visited by many characters from her past. Each person played a part in her story. It seemed some of the people in Grace's life had tried to shield her by building up walls to protect her. But others were building walls to contain her.

In Grace's mind she had locked herself in her Sidan tower to save others from her negative karma. She had thrown away the key long ago while sitting by Kid Flash's bedside when she was only fourteen. She had victimized herself by assuming everything that had happened to her, was her own fault.

But did the people in my life perpetuate my spiraling metamorphosis from being an outgoing, energetic, free spirited child into a careful, contained, isolated adult? Who actually talked to me about all that had happened? Back in those days, folks just didn't speak about the horrible. You were just supposed to work it out yourself. Even her psychiatrist couldn't convince young Grace Ruby to expel her demons. The "lie" became her rock, her foundation. The lie was what Grace built her Sidan tower upon. And now, she was finally feeling the need to break free. But she needed help.

Whose face was that? Whose face was driving the car straight towards my tower of lies? Who was the person that had the key to help me unlock the truth to set me free?

In Grace's dream, the driver of the car had two faces that shifted from one to the other. One was Kid Flash and the other was her neighbor, Michael.

They are the same person!

Grace threw the covers back and sprang out of bed.

"BB, are you awake? It's time to figure out a mystery. Wake up kitty-kitty, wake up," Grace sang out as she prepared for her day...a new day.

⁓つ

Seven-thirty A.M., Grace was hungry, really hungry. She pulled some bread from the freezer and beat two eggs to make French toast. BB crunched on his kitty kibble while Grace worked in the kitchen.

Today she needed to do some research. She needed to check the old records to see what was said about the accident that she and Michael were involved in. There was only so much she could remember. After the hospital, everything sort of washed away with the tide.

She also needed to look through her grandmother's records. Grace wasn't even sure of the date that her mother passed on, or whether she had even returned to Lowel to finish her sophomore year. It seemed that the period of time, in which Grace worked on becoming introverted, had left a dead spot in her memory.

And she needed to check on the name Michael Berkshire. Perhaps there was some kind of article or report on the boy's condition in the *Mill Valley Herald* archives, or the Marin County Sheriff's Office.

One thing was for sure, she knew in her heart that Michael was Kid Flash and he was alive and well. That fact alone felt like a giant redwood tree was lifted off her shoulders. All those years of guilt and the boy was right under her watchful eye the whole time—fit and healthy.

But did he know who I was? If he did, why didn't he come forward years before? Or was he just as desperate to keep secrets as much as I was?

Grace hoped that she hadn't scared Michael away with her odd and emotional behavior. Today was a new day, and Grace Ruby was a bit more prepared to listen to some answers. She wondered what a man did on his first morning of retirement.

Grace got up and made a second batch of buttery French toast. She pulled down some little Chinese take-out boxes that she had for when it was her turn to bring lunch for her gardening group. She cut the French toast into small triangles and packed them into the bottom with a sprinkling of powdered sugar. In another box she put some cut up cantaloupe and green grapes. She heated up some syrup in the microwave and poured it into a little glass jar that she had saved and wrapped it in a tiny tea towel. She packed everything into one of her reusable grocery bags and sat down to add a note.

Rapunzel has gone mad
Eat this to restore her sanity

She slipped on her orange sandals and delivered the gift to his door. Like an excited teen, she rang the bell and ran.

Twenty-Nine

There is something 'bout hope
That freshens a day
Like clothes on the line
Or rain in May
It ignites a joy
That fuels the heart
And chases the demons away

~⁓

"Hello, yes this is the County Sheriff's Department."

"Yes, I'm interested in a car accident report from December 1966, involving a burgundy Pontiac GTO." Grace was anxious.

"Well, that was certainly a long time ago," the voice responded with a smidgen of suspicion. "May I ask why?"

"Well, I was the one in the accident and there may have been a fatality."

"May have?" The lady's voice was now dripping with skepticism.

"I was very young, but now I would like to read what happened, exactly," Grace made her voice sound calm, not crazed.

"I see. Well, you're going to have to come down to the station for that kind of information," the lady added. She sounded like there was a call waiting on another line, and she needed to end the one with Grace.

"Oh, all right then. Thank you very much."

Grace hung up the phone in slow motion. She still had a land line along with a cell phone.

What was it exactly that I wanted to know? I already learned about Michael Berkshire three things: one, he was alive and well, two, he obviously had kept my secret or I would have been in jail, and three, if he was deranged and dangerous, I wouldn't be here.

No, now I want to know about the child that was hit. Was she the little white haired girl that I had seen earlier that fateful night, or was it someone else? Or did I really hit a deer and not a person. Or even better, maybe there was no accident at all and I had simply gone insane for a period of time after my father's passing and my mother's prognosis.

But Grace didn't drive. She would have to call for a driver to take her back to Mill Valley.

Knock, knock, knock!

BB jumped off Grace's lap and headed for the bedroom.

"Now, who could that be?" Grace whispered with hope oozing from her cheery mood. She got up to peek out of the tiny hole in her front door and crossed her fingers.

There he stood with an arm full of orange hibiscus flowers and greenery. Grace could barely make out Michael's face behind the blooms. She opened the door and smiled.

"Thank you for breakfast. And you even deliver," he said as he offered her his gift.

"It's the least I could do for a man of leisure," Grace said, while stepping aside so he could enter.

"I also wanted to apologize for my hasty retreats the last few days," she added.

"Who's this?" Michael asked when he spotted Grace's kitten cautiously coming out to check on their guest. "You kept him. I'm so glad."

"This is BB and he's my angel."

Grace reached over and gathered the flowers in her arms so Michael could squat down and coax the kitten over to him. The tall man got down to floor level and wiggled his fingers by his shoe. BB crouched down in the attack position and kicked his little paws until he got traction on Grace's hardwood floors. Then the little ball of orange fur skidded over to the giant man and started playing.

"He likes you."

"Yes, he remembers me. I rescued him from the back alley."

Grace got a vase and started arranging.

"I won't keep you," Michael said as he stepped up behind her. Grace felt like he was electrically charged. He wasn't even touching her, but she could still feel him inches from her back.

"I was wondering, if tonight perhaps, you would like to walk with me to dinner so that we can talk," he asked. His tone was sultry and cautious.

Grace nodded yes without turning around.

Her stomach actually dropped. She was torn between conflicting emotions. She wanted to know everything, but then again she didn't. *Is he going to accuse me of the lie that I told over forty-five years ago? Or is he going to offer forgiveness? Is it comforting to know that he lived so close, or is it disturbing? And, is this fire that I feel for him, just a crazy old lady crush from a teenage memory, or is it the climax to a long and complicated vague love affair?*

"Six then?" he asked as he headed for the door.

Grace didn't answer, but instead began to breathe again when she heard the door click shut.

After a quick shower, Grace got dressed and called for a driver. She always used Abio's on Chestnut. They were a limo service that also had a fleet of smaller, comfortable cars. Her favorite driver was Jeremy and he was available.

BB was asleep on his spot on the bed. *What a little dolly he is.* Grace could not imagine her life without him. How quickly things were changing. She hadn't even discussed her admission out loud yet, but already she was feeling better. And today, hopefully, she could get a few answers, as well.

Jeremy arrived at ten sharp. It was only a few miles to Mill Valley but it was a Tuesday, mid-morning, and traffic along 101 would be thick.

Grace never learned to drive after her accident. In fact, she tried to stay out of cars altogether. That was one of the best things about living in the city—she could get around without needing her own car—cable cars, busses, taxis, but mainly walking; that suited her perfectly. Still, getting into a car made her nervous. Her doctor had prescribed something for anxiety that she took when she traveled. Grace got some juice and took two. She was definitely anxious today.

"All set?" Jeremey asked when he was sure Grace was buckled in tight. He knew that riding in cars made her uneasy.

"Yes. You have the address I gave you?"

"Yes Miss," he answered.

Grace closed her eyes as Jeremy maneuvered through the Marina District traffic.

"At the Golden Gate, Miss," he announced. He also knew that she loved it when the ocean and bay were visible.

Grace opened her eyes and started breathing in big breaths of air. She rolled down her window to let the salty breeze into the car.

The morning fog was just beginning to lift and she could see steamers coming into the bay filled with crates. The ocean below looked solid. No white caps or ripples. The Pacific looked like a blue-green carpeted expanse that was continuous and unbroken. Grace could feel the tightness in her spine loosening as she kept her eyes on her childhood horizon. Sometimes the ocean felt more stable than the ground that she lived on. Grace rolled up the window and closed her eyes as the car exited the bridge and entered Sausalito.

"May I help you?"
Grace stepped up to the window.

"Yes, I called yesterday. I'm looking for some information regarding a possible fatality involving a car accident on Highway One in December of 1966.

"I see. That would be in our archive department. Let me call back there and see if anyone is available to help."

"Thank you very much." Grace went and sat down on one of the wooden benches along the wall. She didn't have to wait long.

"Ma'am, my name's Brad Heller. Follow me please."

Grace followed Brad to the back of the building to a room stacked high with file folders and boxes. The room felt sad and smelled musty.

"I believe the records go back that far. My team has been working for months on transferring these written reports into our database. Have a seat, please."

Brad was small and wiry. He had curly, light red hair and trendy horn rimmed glasses.

He logged in.

"Give me all the details that you can," he said without looking up from his keyboard.

"Well, it was in December of 1966. It involved a '65 or '66 burgundy Pontiac GTO. There were two teens in the vehicle. One of them was me, Grace Ruby Van Vliet. That's all I remember." Grace fibbed a bit.

Brad clicked his fingers along the keys while Grace looked down at her lap. Her fingers were tightly entwined with one another. She subconsciously was praying intensely for a miracle.

"Hmmm."

Hmmm what? Thought Grace.

Brad seemed to take an eternity before he answered.

"Seems there was a disfigurement along with a death."

Grace's heart was pounding.

"Let's go look in the evidence box."

Grace's stomach lurched as Brad pushed back his chair and got up.

"Hmmm, let's see. Oh yes, I will need to get the ladder."
Grace followed him from one row of stacked boxes to another.
"Here it is." Brad rolled the connecting ladder to the area where Grace's nightmare was stored. He climbed the rungs quickly and pulled down the top carton labeled:

DECEMBER 18, 1966 CASE SOLVED
ONE DEATH, PEDESTRIAN
DRUNK DRIVER

"I'll leave you to it, for a bit," Brad said when he saw the look on Grace's face.

Grace Ruby slumped down to the storeroom floor and straddled the box between her knees. She lifted up on the seal and removed the lid. This was it; here it was…her lie, packed perfectly away in a sheriff's department cardboard box. Grace closed her eyes and immediately her mind went back to that foggy moment of impact. She could smell pears and alcohol, she could feel the powerful vibrations coming from the muscle car, she could hear the music pounding into her chest, and she saw what she hit. She saw it all along.

With a tender touch Grace lifted out the little white pea coat. The entire left side was covered in forty-eight-year-old dried blood. The inside lining was frayed and disintegrating. The tag was still attached at the collar: Size 8. The right sleeve was missing entirely.

Grace laid the coat across her lap and reached inside the box. There next was Grace's father's bomber jacket. Grace couldn't believe it. She took her hands and squeezed the soft leather and brought it out and up to her nose. Grace inhaled and the faintest smell of Old Spice filled her heart.

In the bottom of the box was a half empty pack of cigarettes, the GTO hood emblem, a pack of Black Jack chewing gum, and the lie upholding, empty bottle of Pear Ripple.

Grace's whole being suddenly felt covered with sickening guilt. The weight of her past pressed her to the ground. With shaking arms, she lifted the little girl's coat off her lap and placed it back in the box. She took her father's jacket and slipped it on and began sobbing. She really had never grieved, not for her father, her mother, the little girl in the white pea coat, or herself. Grace had never grieved the death of her true self. The box in front of her became a coffin.

Grace stood up and slipped her hands into her cheating father's coat pockets. The anger was still there, but it was fading, such conflicting emotions of resentment and sad love. Grace pushed her hands into the pockets deeper and felt something hard.

What is this? she thought, as she pulled out a tiny block of wood.

"Jeremey, please take me to Marin General Hospital next," Grace said as she got into the back seat of the car.

"Are you ill, Miss?" he asked with concern.

"No, no, I'm looking for some information about something that happened a long, long time ago." Grace's voice trailed off.

Grace Ruby blew her nose and fiddled with her make-up as they moved along Almenar Drive. Now, to see if there were records on Michael Berkshire, Grace was pretty sure MG was the hospital that they both had been taken to.

After the police had discovered their overturned car, Grace really didn't remember much. She had been in shock from the trauma. It seemed there was an ambulance, and a gurney, but other than that, her memory was blank.

"I'll drop you off here," Jeremey said as they neared the front entrance. "Just call me on your cell phone when you're ready to go, and I'll come back right here to pick you up. You still have my number, don't you?"

"Yes, yes," Grace answered. She really hated cell phones. She hated that she could be gotten hold of at any time. Most days, she just left the thing in her house on purpose.

"Alright then, just call," he said kindly.

~

Grace loathed hospitals. Hospitals were germy. Sure they helped people, but they also made people sick, as well. Grace reached into her purse and squirted hand sanitizer onto her fingertip after pushing the elevator button. The administration offices were on the third floor. Grace held her breath while going up the elevator. There were two people riding with her.

"I am looking for some information on a past patient of this hospital," Grace inquired at the front desk.

"Are you family?"

Oh dear, do I speak yet another lie?

"No, this is a case from forty years ago," is what came out of Grace's mouth. "The patient and I were in an accident together and he was horribly injured. I never knew what became of him."

Grace put on her best, frail old-lady voice to invite sympathy. The last part was a lie, but a small one. Plus, she still wasn't one hundred percent sure it was him.

"I see. Well, this sounds like something out of a mystery novel. Hey, are you the lady that writes those detective books with Lord Byron?" The desk girl got perky.

"Yes," Grace usually didn't like to reveal herself, but in this case, she hoped it would help, "why yes I am."

"I love your books! Let's see. Can you tell me the patient's name?"

Grace went through all of the details with the young woman. She kept getting up from behind her desk and going back and forth to some back room.

"Do you remember his doctor's name?" she asked.

"No, I don't."

"Was he a resident of Marin County?"

"Yes, I believe his family was from Mill Valley, like me," Grace offered hopefully.

After around thirty minutes, the girl came flying out of the back.

"I have it, I have it! Michael Berkshire was in here for one hundred and eighty days. He had thirteen surgeries, and seven blood transfusions. He was transferred to San Francisco Mercy for reconstructive work on June 17, 1967." The girl was practically shouting; she was so excited to have solved the mystery.

Grace gave her a huge smile and thanked her over and over for all of her good detective work. She even gave her a signature.

But the gravity of knowing that what she did had resulted in a young man's suffering for six months and longer, made Grace's smile feel plastic and fake.

She turned to call Jeremy on her cell phone after wiping the keys with sanitizer.

~∂

On the drive back to San Francisco, Grace knew that she had one more mystery to solve. But today was not the day. The rest of this day needed to be focused on Michael. No more running away from him. No more distant waving. Tonight she was bound for confessional, no matter what the cost.

As Jeremey opened the car door for her, Grace slipped him a huge tip.

"This is too much, Miss."

"No, please keep it. You were a comfort to me today."

Then Grace did something unexpected. She reached out and hugged the young man tightly.

"Oh my, Miss. Thank you, thank you so much," he said as he chuckled at her outburst of unusual affection.

Grace waved as she climbed the stairs.

BB was at the door when Grace opened it. He bounded over to her and started meowing. Grace reached down, picked him up, and cuddled him to her.

"You are such a teacher of love, aren't you, little one?" Grace said softly.

BB answered in purrs and kitty nose licks.

It was almost three in the afternoon. It was tea-time. Grace filled the kettle and heated it on the stove. She got the canned milk from the fridge and the clover honey from the pantry.

This is a ritual that I would like to keep, thought Grace.

She pulled down her favorite teacup, the one with the chip in it, *such a beautiful, delicate work of art, even with its flaw. Does this cup represent me and my life?*

I did continue to function, even with my horrible secret. I worked, I survived. But for all of these years, I felt ugly on the inside because of my flaws. Is it possible that a mistake can be overlooked or forgiven? Is it okay to break a vow of penance, when the offender truly seeks absolution? Can an imperfection be mended by grace?

Grace came out of her thoughts as the teakettle began its rattle. She lifted it off the stove before the loud whistle sounded.

Today, this day, Grace lifted the cup to her mouth and put her lips right over the chip and took a sip. The tea did not taste sour or bitter; stronger or weaker, in fact, it tasted perfectly perfect, in spite of the teacup's flaw.

Thirty

Kid Flash
You're faster than fast
You hook into the Speed Force
To make your powers last
You think you are invincible
As you speed down Highway One
A super human speed demon
Oh no, look what you've done!

Five P.M., time to get ready. Grace had not been this nervous in a long time. In all of her adult life, she had never gone out on a date. Oh, she knew all about dates and what to do; she had not been living in a cave. In fact, as a writer, she went into great detail about all the particulars of love. But the very last real and passionate kiss, that she herself had received, was from the man she was seeing tonight, and that was forty-eight years ago!

Really, what was she thinking? Grace looked at herself in the bathroom mirror. Her eyes were dull and lined. There were tiny wrinkles at the corners of her mouth. She kept her adult self out of the sun, but still there were dark spots and patches on her skin. Her chest area was heading south. As fit as she was, she had a tummy. Her best features were her dancer's legs and her long hair. Both were not the same as last year, or the year before that. Her body (her teacup) was chipped, but could it still do the job? She felt today it could.

Grace had carefully observed her neighbor over the many years without knowing who he was. She had watched his hair turn and his shape age. But none of that had mattered to her. Watching him move through time was a privilege that Grace had enjoyed secretly from her living room window. Even through their twenties, thirties, forties, fifties, and now sixties, with each wave, Grace's heart would skip a beat.

Grace Ruby understood that even if the body changes, passion does not have to wane. Age was not an indicator of romantic fire. When Michael had grabbed her and pulled her to him the night before, Grace had felt fourteen, once again. It was all she could do not to burst into flames. With his overtures the last few days, it seemed Michael felt the same way.

Grace decided her nervousness was about the conversation that they were going to have. But the excitement she felt was all about passion. Grace was waking up from a long, dormant, personality sleep. Her extroverted self was beginning to rouse, and passion was helping to soothe the pain.

~

Six o'clock exactly, knock, knock, knock.

Grace took one more look in the mirror. Tonight she wore a long, Greek blue Tahari skirt and a simple, dark gray tank with a matching wrap. She put her hair in a loose updo. She wore light make-up and a touch of gloss. She decided against a fragrance and just hoped the lemon verbena soap wouldn't be too strong. Since they were walking, she slipped on her orange sandals.

She picked up BB and opened the door.

Oh my, he looked amazing. Dark-wash jeans, white open collared shirt, and black blazer.

"You look beautiful, Grace Ruby," he said, as he took little BB from her arms and held the kitten in his cupped hands.

Grace didn't know what to say. All of a sudden, everything was throwing her introverted self off. She started to have a mild panic attack as she looked at the complicated man standing before her, holding her kitty. He looked so strong, so normal, so different.

Once again, like when she was a teen, Grace had a feeling of apprehension. But instead of stepping away, she stepped closer.

"Michael, you look so different from my memory of you. Are you the boy that loved speed, cars, and fried clams?"

Michael bent down and put BB on the floor. Then he reached up and moved his hair away from his forehead and from around his temples. He leaned into Grace's vision and she could see long, jagged scars where the skin met the hair line. Then he turned around and lifted his hair off his neck and pulled his collar down. Grace could see massive scar tissue.

"Yes, little girl," he said as he turned back to her. "It's me. I'm Kid Flash and I've wanted to apologize to you for four decades."

What? What did he just say? Grace went into a bit more shock as she fumbled for her keys to lock the door.

How could this be? What did he have to apologize for? He read my manuscript; he knows that I lied to the police by incriminating him. He did nothing wrong, except for meeting me!

"Let's save all of that for later," Michael said, as he helped Grace with her wrap.

"It's a beautiful spring evening in the most romantic city on the entire planet. Let's just enjoy walking side by side for the very first time," Michael added.

It was a gorgeous dusk. The sun was just beginning to rest its head down onto its watery ocean bed. There always was the tiniest of lulls between six and seven in the evening in San Francisco. It was as if all of the pedestrians would duck into the nearest building and nap. The city seemed tamer, more melancholy than at any other hour of the day. Tonight was clear and perfect.

Michael offered his arm when they reached the bottom of the stairs. Grace slipped hers into his just as natural as could be.

Grace leaned into him as they headed up Hyde.

"Let's take Lombard," Grace said.

"Alright, I haven't done that in years. I used to bring the kids there when they were small."

Grace pictured the children in the photos in Michael's home. Such sweet faces.

"My garden club has been doing some planting on the east side," Grace said, as she pulled him over to the top railing.

The hydrangeas were budding against a lime green background of spring leaves. The tourist stream was light. Grace started telling Michael about each plant and how hard it was to maintain the precise planting patterns year after year. Every bush had its exact place.

"I like the rules that the Historical Horticulture Society has us follow. Everything is orderly."

Michael leaned his ear close to her lips as they maneuvered each of the eight hairpin turns. He never once looked out at the views.

"And that is how the Stairway Project began," Grace said, as they exited onto Leavenworth.

Michael stopped her and drew her into his arms for an embrace.

He was tall, but so was she. Grace felt like they fit together perfectly.

"Come on, this gardening talk has made me hungry," Michel said, as he pulled away and they started up yet another steep road.

~

"Oh my, oh my. Non posso crederci! I can't believe it!" Giovanni grabbed Grace and exclaimed. "How beautiful you are on the arm of a man!"

Grace was so glad that Michael had decided to take her to her very favorite Italian restaurant. It wasn't her usual day, but that did not bother her. She asked for a private table away from the main dining room.

"Lo portero una bottiglia di vino dell casa," Giovanni said after seating the couple in a romantic, secluded corner of the trattoria.

When he brought the bottle of wine to the table, he gave Grace Ruby a wink and a giant Italian warm smile.

Grace still couldn't believe that she was sitting across from her handsome neighbor. The man she had watched vicariously, as he lived his vibrant life. And now, the amazing coincidence that he was the boy that had survived the accident that Grace had caused, back in December of 1966. *Why didn't you come up to me?*

"I have so many questions, and so much to ask you, that I don't even know where to begin," Grace spoke softly while looking down at the table.

"Well, first let's have a toast," Michael whispered as he raised his glass. "To the past we cannot change, the future we can mold, and the present that is perfect."

They clinked their wine glasses together and took sips, Grace savored the present moment before either end of time was discussed and revealed.

"Well, let's start with the past first," Grace Ruby offered. "What do you remember about that night?"

"Well I remember that afternoon, perfectly. I was minding my own business, clearing the carburetor on my new car, when up the driveway walks this sassy little girl with long legs and long blonde hair."

Giovanni placed some crostini covered with olive tapenade on the table. Michael and Grace both took a few bites before Michael went on.

"The following day, I was going down to enlist for the war. I didn't want to risk getting drafted. My parents had splurged and bought me the Pontiac for my eighteenth Birthday. I loved that car more than anything. They promised that they would have it waiting for me when I returned. It was weird, because I was sadder leaving that car behind than I was leaving my whole family.

"But then I saw you. You were the most beautiful girl I had ever seen; tall and confident, and mouthy...I liked that. You looked wild, and like trouble. I honestly thought that you wouldn't show that night."

Grace looked up and Giovanni was standing there waiting for direction.

"Maestro, will you just pick your favorites and dazzle us, per favore, il mio amico?"

"Of course bell signora, of course."

"After you left," Michael continued, "I couldn't get you out of my thoughts. In my mind, you were going to be the girl I dreamed of every night when I went off to Nam. You would be the girl that I came home to. I didn't even know you, but that's how the eighteen year old mind of a boy works, I guess.

"So, when you showed up, it took every ounce of strength I had to remain cool and aloof. But I was excited. I was excited to introduce you to my first love, my GTO. For some reason, I knew that you were the girl that would truly appreciate my perfect machine, and you were. Bomber jacket, jeans, even that little piece of wood you kept fiddling with...all of it was so sexy."

Grace was blushing now. Her cheeks felt hot from the candle. She drank some ice water and pushed back from the table to fan herself.

"And then you were screaming. It was amazing. I felt so powerful—so invincible as we were heading up the coast. You weren't afraid. It was almost as if living and dying were just the same to you; that you wanted to just be in the moment with me! I felt so lucky to be having a wild night of memories with you and my car.

"Here it is...I knew who you were. I knew who your family was. I knew how old you were. I just didn't care. You were going to be my best memory ever. Kid Flash was using his super power speed to catch a girl, a wild girl"

Grace's mind was racing. *I just can't believe this. All of this time, I felt the villain. But I am the villain. It doesn't matter what he knew. I'm the reckless one, not him!*

Giovanni brought their soup, a tiny cup of stracciatella. Michael refilled Grace's wine glass.

"Go on," Grace said quietly.

"When you asked to drive, I thought my heart was going to explode, you, this amazing, hot girl, driving my car? Holy cow! You were such a baby, so young. I thought that I was going to have to teach you how to drive, but you just picked it up right away. Incredible! It was almost like the car liked you, as well."

Grace would have interrupted, but she had already let him into her private thoughts by having him read the manuscript of her memoir.

Everything seemed so different now with his perspective out in the open. If he was a vegetable living in some institution, or worse yet, dead...she never would have known his view. Grace would still be locked in her nightmare prison, alone. Grace's memory of the night was gaining depth.

"Then the fog rolled over onto the highway, and I had a moment of, 'this isn't good'. But we were almost back and the alcohol had taken effect. I was looking at your beautiful face when you floored the GTO. Your eyes were wild with exhilaration. I kept thinking of the kiss we had shared. I was storing everything about the evening up for my future dreams when..."

Michael paused.

"Let's take a break," he said, "I'm curious to see what the next course will be. No wonder you love this place."

Grace's heart was pounding. The next part of the story would be excruciating. She wondered if he had told anyone else this part of his history; his parents, his wife perhaps. Grace had a flash of the boy she remembered going around and around in the front area of the car. *Did he have the same memory of me? Did he see what I hit? Did he see who I hit?*

Grace pushed her scaloppini around on her plate. The last thing that she wanted to do now was eat.

Michael took a few bites of his food and turned his head to look out into the main part of the restaurant. He had a faraway look and demeanor, like he needed to dip back into the pain to be able to find the perfect descriptive words.

"I saw her."

He paused again and chewed his bite. His head was still facing away from Grace.

"I thought she was a ghost, an omen of what awaited me in Vietnam. I didn't think she was real. She turned and saw the car coming at her. It was all so fast. The first seconds I thought, 'How did we hit a ghost?' but then the car started rolling and you flew out of the driver's seat and I felt you hit my back…"

Big tears were streaming out of Grace's eyes. She didn't move, she didn't breathe.

"I thought that I had killed you. I felt horrible guilt. I was an adult taking a minor on some sort of fantasy joy ride. I could see your hair flailing around as my beautiful GTO was flipping and flipping and then…"

Michael turned to look at her and brought his hand to his face.

"Then I disappeared."

Grace wiped at the tears on her cheeks with her cloth napkin. The two of them just looked at each other for a few minutes.

"Did you know that some people can hear what is being said to them when they are in a coma? I did. I could hear the doctors saying that I would never be the same. I could hear my mother wailing and praying. I could hear my brothers being angry at my situation. I could hear the police whispering.

"Then I heard a tiny voice speak about penance, and never allowing love into their heart. And I thought, 'Thank God, she's alive.' Then it came to me...you were blaming yourself for what happened. I laid there and started to scream at you, 'No, no!' But you couldn't hear me, I couldn't move. The bandages around my face were locking me in like a prison. All the pain that I was in, doubled."

Grace's mind raced back to the visit that she made to Michael in his room at the hospital. She had no idea that he could hear her. *How could he possibly blame himself for what I did?*

"You heard me?" Grace squeaked out.

"Yes, and then you were gone."

Giovanni quietly cleared their plates from the table.

"Era il cibo va bene?" Giovanni asked

"Yes friend, the food was amazing. We are just catching up. Dessert, please?" Grace reached out and touched the restaurant owner's arm.

"Of course, Bella."

"After that," Michael continued, "I spiraled downhill. I almost died a few times, they said. When I finally woke up and I asked for a mirror, well, I just went to a very dark place. I was in the hospital for months having surgery after surgery. I kept waiting for the police to come and take me away so I could die there, and escape all of the physical and emotional pain that I was in. And I kept waiting for you to come and visit me. But they said you had been taken away."

"Taken away where?" Grace asked.

"To the institution."

"The institution?"

"Yes, for the mentally insane," he answered.

Thirty-One

Tragedy Trauma
The Whirly Twirly
Kind of Crazy
That pulls you into a world of
Hazy
Where nothing You can do
Can Make Yesterday
Anew
And prison time is LOONEY time
Within your private zoo

⁓

*G*race froze. *What did he just say? Oh no, oh no, oh no.*
Memories started flooding Grace's being; drenching her like the stormy day her father flew over her head and changed her life. Torrential, pouring, painful memories of hallways and medication, locked doors and stale smoke. She saw her mother and aunt leaving her. She could see the backs of their heads walking towards the car from a barred window; screaming girls in the night, talking sessions, runny eggs, sleeping.

How long was I there, days, months, years?

They kept asking her a question. *What was it?* Grace remembered she never answered it.

Hmmm, oh yes, now I remember.

"How are you dealing with the death of...?"

Grace Ruby had to think for a moment. *Oh yes.*

How are you dealing with the bloody, decapitated, lie filled death of little...Robin Rose?

~9

Grace suddenly felt weary. She signaled Giovanni to bring the bill. Her head was spinning with this new revelation.

"I think that I am ready to go home," Grace said as she looked down at her plate.

"Yes, of course, I'll call for a cab," Michael agreed.

On the short ride back down the hill, both Grace and Michael were quiet. Michel looked drained.

"I hope I didn't say something that upset you," Michael said as they stood at the bottom of Grace's stairway after leaving the cab.

My whole life is upsetting, Grace thought.

"I just need to think about everything. There are some shadows in my history; some things that I just don't remember. I need to sit alone and sort out some fuzzy memories."

Michael nodded and reached out and took Grace's hand. Tenderly he lifted her palm and placed it on his cheek.

"You never got to really know my old face, but I hope my new one isn't too distracting. I think we both need to sit with the truth and the gravity of the things that have shown up in our lives. As for December, 1966 that was not your fault, it was not my fault...it was an accident, a horrible, tragic accident."

Michael dropped his hand to his side and Grace walked up the stairs alone. When she reached the top, she turned around and he was standing there looking up at her. With his usual flair, her handsome neighbor gave her a little four 'o clock wave. Grace Ruby smiled and then went inside.

Bang! Grace slammed her front door and leaned her back up to it. Panic and anxiety took over her body. She started taking in big gulps of air, and then the tears started coming. Grace slumped to the floor and started wailing. In the moment, she couldn't even think. She was just a vessel of hormonal emotions that were roiling and boiling over. Little BB came to his human cautiously and crawled up on her lap. Grace just let her fingers run through his fur as she sobbed and sobbed.

E leven P.M. Grace went to bed and dreamed.
"No, no lady, not that one!" a tiny voice said behind her back.

Grace Ruby was sitting at a table with a freshly stacked Sidan game in front of her.

Every time she went to pull out a block, the voice behind her would tell her that piece was the wrong one. Grace tried again.

"This one?" Grace asked as she went to touch a piece near the top.

"No, no, not that one either."

Grace was getting frustrated. She stood up and looked around the room. It was stark white and full of girls she didn't know. They all seemed to have the same unkempt hair and vacant stare. Then suddenly the girls all began to age right before her eyes. Their faces withered and their wild manes grayed.

Grace walked over to one of the women. And the voice behind her said, "No, no lady, not that one." She tried to turn around to see who was speaking but she couldn't turn quickly enough. Grace walked over to another and the voice said the same thing.

Grace went back and sat down at the puzzle table. Now each block had a word written on one side.

TRAUMA CHALLENGE HOPE SPIRAL CRAZY GRACE FAITH HEALING

122

Grace Ruby reached out for the one with her name on it, GRACE, and paused. "This one?" she asked her invisible guide.

"Of course," said the tiny voice.

Then a delicate, pale hand wrapped around Grace's hand to help steady Grace as she gently tugged at the puzzle piece from the very bottom.

~~~

Grace woke up with a new mental energy. She lay in bed for a while, letting memories come to her. That vague feeling of missing history began clearing as she allowed her mind to relax and not react to what she remembered.

When she had made the conscious decision to lie, her younger psyche had gone into such a deep hiding place that her spirit had shut down completely. Grace remembered that she stopped talking all together; so afraid that she would slip up and everyone would know that she was the one who had killed the girl. She had begun soothing herself by putting everything in order, obsessively. Her sweaters had to be folded just so, her bed made perfectly, her medications had needed to be dispensed in order of their color; lightest to darkest. Grace had started spiraling down into a vortex of controlling her physical world, while ignoring any human interference with that world. In other words, she had gone a little mad.

She must have been in the mental ward for three years, because she remembered three different Christmas mornings around the same artificial tree. By the third Christmas, her mother did not come. That must have been the year she passed away. Grace would have been seventeen.

In all that time, Grace Ruby had assumed Kid Flash had either died, or was living in his own crazy ward as a vegetable. Occasionally she would pray a devilish prayer, hoping the boy was still keeping her secret. That was just one of the many layers of guilt that young, incarcerated Grace had put on herself. Praying to be hidden, praying to disappear and be unnoticed. She had said her prayer at exactly nine at night. Nine exactly.

~9

Grace threw back the covers.
Now where is that thing? Where did I put it? Grace didn't bother with her slippers, she just marched down the hallway to a little used closet where she kept some of her favorite smaller things left to her by her grandmother.

It had been years since Grace had gone through the closet. Most of Grandmother's things were still out and displayed in the home.

Grandmother Van Vliet had been a tasteful woman, a descendant of Louis Van Vliet, the famous chess master. At one time, Grandmother's home had been every socialite's dream. Important people had dined and entertained in the house on Chestnut. It was imperative to Grace's grandmother to have everything just so. The quality of the furnishings had surpassed anything that Grace could ever purchase. Each piece had a timeless, elegant feel that never went out of style. Grace was comforted by the generational stability of her grandmother's aura, so she had changed little.

The smaller, personal things that had been close to her grandmother's heart were stored in the hall closet.

BB wound his way around and between Grace's feet as she stood before the crowded shelves.

Ah, I see the other tea set. Oh and there are my father's baby shoes and the box filled with his primary school papers.

Grace's mind flooded with a memory of seeing her grandmother placing a ruby colored rose on her father's coffin. Grace Ruby could see her grandmother's black gloved arm stretch out over the box and release the bloom.

How horrible that moment must have been for grandmother. To entomb your only son, and then watch as a beautiful, full bloom falls into an open grave to be buried forever. Why did I not notice her pain? There are so many things that you miss, when you are ten, thought Grace as she moved her grandmother's long, black gloves to the side.

Grace pulled out a few more boxes filled with mothballs and tissue paper. One box was labeled GRACE RUBY VAN VLIET. Grace knew this box well.

When she first moved in with her grandmother, permanently, Grace had discovered the treasure box by accident. Grandmother had asked Grace to retrieve a set of good silver to teach young Grace how to polish correctly. When she had lifted the silver set off the shelf, her name had caught her eye.

In it were many of her baby things, objects that had been taken from the cottage after her mother's passing. There were clam shells and painted pinecones. A worn copy of *Charlotte's Web*, a faded piece of a pink baby's blanket, a small red ball and jacks, a soft baby doll, a handmade card to Mommy, and a few photos of Grace sitting on the beach holding a clam shovel.

Today, as she held the treasure box in her arms, Grace realized that it was her grandmother, her father's mother that came to pick her up from the institution. She was the one that had taken over her care after her three-year mental breakdown.

Wasn't it always Grandmother who came to my rescue? She must have offered to continue my education and rehabilitation from home. Maybe the mental ward that I was in was part of the prison system, and I HAD been charged with some sort of manslaughter? Maybe everyone knew all along that I was the driver?

There were so many more questions that Grace needed answers for, but everyone was dead by now; except for Michael Berkshire. Grace needed to ask him two important questions. One: did he receive prison time for something that he didn't even do? And two: did he know that she had lied and blamed him?

Graced moved a few more things around in her treasure box.

Ah, there it is.

Grace gently removed one of the two Sidan games from her past, and took the puzzle into her study to set it up.

Little BB followed close behind Grace's feet. It seemed every part of his new home was exciting. Grace could tell that he liked the study because there were papers to rustle and pencils to bat. *And now his human had a tall box with things inside that rattled,* thought Grace. *Very fun.*

Grace pulled up her grandmother's antique arts and crafts desk chair to the table and opened the Sidan box. A smell of *life before* wafted into the room when she opened the flaps. In her mind she could see her father sitting across from her, waiting patiently for her to stack the blocks while smoke curled up and out of his pipe.

"Keep steady, Ruby Gem, never let anything rattle you," Grace heard her father say.

Grace began to stack. She placed each block a little bit differently; some close together and others with a slight gap.

Keep steady, Grace said to herself as she added layer after layer. It was amazing how easy it was to get back in the rhythm of building.

"Never let anything rattle you," this Grace said out loud. "Never let anything rattle you?"

The tower was getting higher and higher. With each layer, Grace said the mantra: "Never let anything rattle you, never let anything rattle you," louder and louder.

Until she was almost to the top and she shouted, "I did what you said, I did what you said! I've stayed calm, I've stayed in control. It was you! You were the one not in control. How could you, how could you?" Grace was yelling now and just as she added the last piece, the whole tower tumbled down and spilled out onto the floor.

BB dashed around, pawing the pieces on the hard wood floors while Grace pushed back the desk chair and stormed to the closet to get the other Sidan box, the one with words.

In the second box of Sidan there were blocks with words written on them. Grace's father had carefully printed various words to help her with reading and spelling. There were fifty-four blocks in a box. Each time she and her father would play, Grace had the opportunity to learn fifty-four words.

Grace sat the box on the desk and got down on the floor to scoop up the other Sidan pieces. BB helped by pushing the little blocks of wood towards Grace.

Amongst all of Grace's outbursts and wails of sorrow, her new little friend continued to be happy and comforting. Grace gathered up the kitten and scratched his head and under his chin. He answered her with his surprisingly loud purr and snuggled back. Grace could feel herself calming.

"You are my angel, aren't you, little one?" Grace whispered.

After the spilled game parts were put back in the box, Grace dumped out the older set onto the desk. She felt her father's spirit wash over her as she touched and read the words that he had meticulously written. Colors and names of things found in Muir Woods, names and other nouns, descriptive words and feelings, words that became such integral parts of her storytelling in her Lord Byron novels.

Grace flipped each block so that the words were facing up. Next she lined up all of the pieces into rows of six. Just as Grace suspected, there were pieces missing; three pieces.

Grace got up and opened the drapes to her study to let in more light. She walked around and around the "word" history before her.

Hmmm, over and over she had seen and played with these words when she was a child. *Which three are missing?* Grace wrung her hands unconsciously and hummed a melody as she went through the list from memory. *When You Wish Upon a Star,* was the tune.

Then Grace remembered the piece that was in her father's bomber jacket; the tiny block of wood that was lying in the police box coffin in Mill Valley. *Was there a word written on it?* Grace couldn't recall. *And what was it Michael had said at dinner? Something about me fiddling with a piece of wood in the GTO, that must have been the same piece.*

Hmmm, what words are missing?

"Ah ha," Grace said out loud, startling BB. "My name is missing. GRACE is missing."

But what else?

She looked down at the remaining fifty-one blocks. She read:

FERN SORRY OCEAN AZURE HOPE SPIRAL KELP TRAUMA
ROSE COASTAL STRENGTH RUBY FEARLESS LOVE UNLOVED

Graced paused at UNLOVED. *I wonder why he thought I needed to learn that word.*

Grace read some more:

EXPOSED EARTHEN STORM FORGIVENESS KNOWLEDGE BLAND TORMENT

She could hear her father saying, "Try again, Ruby Gem. Sound it out. Good girl."

Over and over she would say the words as she built the tower. Higher and higher her vocabulary would go with each layer of blocks.

"Oh I know, ROBIN is missing, that's it."

Robin? That's strange. Isn't that the name of the little girl I hit?

Grace ran back around to the front of the desk.

Where is it? Where is it?

Grace backed away from the table in shock. Her face had drained of color and she felt sick. There in the middle of the vocabulary list was a four letter word; a word that made the hairs on Grace's neck prickle. The word was…ROSE.

Thirty-Two

We are never really alone, oh
We may shut our doors or crawl into our minds, but
We are all connected by unseen energies, that
We don't understand, because
We are all family, in one way or another.

~~~

Grace needed tea. She needed her adult habit of ritual to calm herself. She needed to heat and steep, pour and sip. Grace needed to think.

With shaking hands Grace pulled down her favorite chipped teacup. She turned the teakettle on and pulled the canned milk from the fridge and the clover honey from the pantry. She did each of these steps without thinking. That was the beauty of precise ritual; it freed the mind from mundane tasks to allow for deeper contemplation.

Even though Grace had suppressed her born nature of being outgoing and extroverted, her trauma induced, controlled, invented, introverted personality had served her well over her adult life.

Being introverted allowed for her professional writing to blossom. She became much more attentive and quizzical. She became an observer of others as they experienced things that she would never dare to do. She developed characters and plots based on study and imagination.

But deep down inside, Grace still longed to run free. She missed her daring nature and only played it out on the pages of her novels. The lie that she told to cover her crime, was like a heavy lid clamped onto a boiling pot of feelings. And now, with all of this new information and revelation, the lid was coming loose and her true nature was beginning to escape…like piping hot steam.

An image of her mother flowed out of the steam from her tea. In this memory/vision Grace saw her mother sitting on the couch by the window in their cottage home. Little Grace was curled up on her mother's lap having her hair stroked.

"Where's Daddy?" asked little Grace Ruby.

"Oh, he's working again," her mother answered with a faraway tone to her voice.

Even at that young age, Grace could tell that she was fibbing.

"You sound sad, Mommy," Little Grace said.

"I just feel all alone, sometimes, that's all, honey,"

"But you have me!" little Grace chimed.

Grace could feel her mother's warm hug in her recollection. But then her mother let her go and stared again out the darkened front window.

~

Crash!

"Oh no, oh no!"

Grace watched in horror as her favorite teacup crashed into the bottom of the sink.

Year after year, afternoon after afternoon Grace had used that exact cup from her grandmother's set. It represented so much to Grace—the classic age that her grandmother came from, the delicate floral pattern, the ritual of civil behavior—but it was the chip that was so endearing. Grace knew that tiny chip represented her true-born given nature. Everyday having sips of tea around, near, or on that tiny flaw—was the way Grace acknowledged, and loved her hidden, suppressed spirit.

And now that spell was broken.

Grace took a breath.

"Coffee, I'm going to make coffee," she announced to BB, who had his little head down in his food bowl, nibbling on his kibble. Grace left the pieces of teacup in the sink and went to look for a thick, sturdy mug.

~~

Grace took the steaming mug and sat down on her tête-a-tête settee. She looked down at her favorite place to sit comfortably. The chair always had been an ironic place for her to rest; a woman that lived alone having a chair for two was definitely eccentric. But was it a clue? There was just something about its symmetry that was eating at her. Grace was missing something.

Maybe it was the way her mind had been wrestling with her duel natures. She remembered being outgoing and unrestrained as a girl, yet now she was a controlled recluse.

Or maybe the chair represents the quiet, natural setting that I grew up in, versus the loud, brightly lit, vibrant city that is now my home. Or could it be that I've been holding onto the chair waiting for my handsome neighbor, Michael, to join my life when the time was just right?

Then Grace's thoughts slowly turned to the flash of memory she had of the twin blonde girls sitting on the beach with their mother. Both little girls had the whitest hair she had ever seen. They were tiny, but looked about six years old. Grace would have been ten when she spotted them sitting by her favorite clam digging spot.

Grace closed her eyes to see the scene more clearly. *An orange blanket, the girls with matching suits, one in blue, the other in pink, the warm sand.* But it was their mother that she now focused on. *The woman seemed to recognize me in some subtle way, and then she turned her head away and looked out to sea.*

In her memory, Grace remembered looking down at her own long, bright white hair.

Vroom, vroom!

"What in the world?"

Vroom, vroom, vroom!

Grace put her coffee down and dug out her opera glasses from between the settee's cushion.

At first she thought it was kids racing down Hyde Street.

Vroom!

Grace stood up, and looked down through her big picture window and couldn't believe her eyes. There, in her handsome neighbor Michael's parking spot, was a deep burgundy, big, thick muscle car with its hood up.

Grace threw the glasses on the chair and ran up to the window. She looked down and could see a side view of Michael with his head close to the engine under the open hood.

Vroom! *Oh my, oh my, what a car!* thought Grace. This was not the tiny foreign sports car that usually sat in front of Michael's home. No, this was a meaty muscle car. Grace's heart was pounding.

Jeans, I must have a pair of jeans around here some place, she thought.

Grace went through her chesterfield and found two pairs. She had bought stretch style jeans for a benefit that had a sixties theme a few years back. One was black and the other dark blue. She tried them both on and the blue fit the best. She pulled on a tee and a black sweater, and then slipped on her orange sandals.

Grace checked on BB, who was curled up on his side of the tête-a-tête settee, and grabbed her house keys. She wasn't even thinking. No planning, no calculating, just moving on instinct. She was excited.

Vroom, the car called to her, awaking her inner child, as she headed down to the street below.

"Hey little girl, what took you so long?"

"Who wants to know?" Grace quipped.

Grace jaywalked across the street towards her neighbor.

"What kind of retirement car is this?" Grace asked, as she admired it from the safety of the sidewalk.

"This, little girl is way too much car for you. It has a 426-horse power, 6.2 liter V8, with a six speed automatic gearbox. It's a retro model of my first Pontiac. So, I am definitely not headed for the rest home, yet."

Grace laughed at that. It felt good to laugh.

When was the last time I laughed? Grace asked herself.

"Want to go for a ride?"

"Oh no, no," Grace's stomach knotted up. "I don't do muscle cars."

"How about just sitting inside and talking?"

Grace looked up and around. San Francisco people were everywhere doing their thing. Tourists and business people, residents and transients, all were swimming up and down Hyde Street like fish in a stream. She and Michael stood perfectly still while the world swirled and eddied around them.

He was standing up at the front of the car, by the passenger door. Grace slipped her hands in her jean pockets and she and Michael locked eyes.

This was a pivotal moment for both of them. Grace imagined Michael was looking at someone who saw his old face, someone who had kissed his original lips. Perhaps he was hoping to have someone in his life that would remember his true self. Grace was embarking on exposing her demons and unleashing the truth, no matter what the consequence. Both of them appeared to take a moment deciding whether to move forward or not.

"Okay, but turn the engine off. Okay?"

Michael smiled and slammed the hood down, and Grace opened the door and got inside.

"Ahhh, I love the smell of a new car. Don't you?" Michael asked as he and Grace shut the noise of the city away.

Grace's hairs on her arms were prickled up, she was nervous.

"Smells like a leather jacket," she answered back. "Is this a GTO?"

"Yes, I couldn't believe it when I heard they were doing a retro version of the car that I once owned."

Grace froze for a moment. She pictured herself standing on a World War II minefield. She wasn't sure whether to go forward, or even where to step. She turned her head and watched a homeless woman pushing an empty baby stroller up the sidewalk. She decided to say nothing.

"Grace, you and I experienced something together that was horrendous."

Michael was turned in the driver's seat so that he could face her.

"I lost months of my life to the hospital, my dream of being a soldier, my youth, my car, even my face, all because I wanted to joyride with a beautiful young girl and show off my car.

"From what I am gathering, you too lost so much because of guilt and the trauma."

Grace was wringing her hands without noticing.

"But a little girl lost her life. An innocent baby wandered onto the highway at the wrong time. In that one instant, three families' lives were catapulted in unimaginable, unplanned directions. I have not slept peacefully since that moment," Michael said.

Grace could barely make out his last few words.

"Were we arrested?" Grace dared to start exploring.

"I was charged with gross vehicle manslaughter. But because of the state of my injuries, I did not do jail time. All of this, I don't remember. It's just the story I was told. Years later, I heard a rumor that you had been institutionalized because of a mental breakdown. I don't believe you were charged of any crime."

"What about the girl's family? Do you know anything about them?" Grace turned in her seat to face Michael.

"All I know is that the mother never pressed further charges against me or my family. It's as if the whole thing faded away."

"Did you know that I lied to the police, and told them you were the one driving?"

There it was. Grace put the question out there. Michael paused as the sentence dangled in the air.

"Yes, yes I did."

Grace was stunned.

"Did you speak up against me?"

"No."

"Why not?"

"Like I said before, I was the adult, I felt responsible. You were just a kid."

"So you mean you kept my horrible secret to yourself all this time?"

"Yes, I did."

Grace looked down at her chest. Her heart was pounding.

"Why?" she finally got out.

"Because I loved you."

What, what? Nobody does something like that because they love someone. Who keeps secrets just because they love someone? There's no such thing as love. My mother and father obviously never loved each other. My aunt never loved me. My father was a cheater. My mother was weak.

"How could you possibly have loved me? We were only together for a couple of hours. I turned on you. I betrayed you. I gave up all that I was to keep my horrible secret intact, with never a thought of you. I was reckless and hurting and so damaged. How could you have loved me?"

"I don't know. I just did. Still do, really.

"When I first moved in on Hyde," Michael continued, "and learned that you were my neighbor, it was all I could do to not go over and knock on your door. But you were so reclusive, and your career was taking off; I didn't want to stir up horrible memories. And I certainly didn't want to talk about the accident. You never gave me any indication that you recognized me or wanted anything to do with me, so I moved on."

"Yes, oh yes, I'm so glad that you did. But I had no idea it was you until the other night. You were just a beautiful life to watch from afar. I observed you like a science experiment. I was wound so tightly in my web of deceit, that the only glimpse of a normal life I had was when I would see you and your family out and about."

Now it was Michael's turn to face away. He lifted both hands and put them on the wheel.

"You really didn't recognize me, did you?" he said. His voice was soft and emotional.

"No, I didn't. Even when you told me your name, I didn't believe it."

"I guess we are the same then. You hid in your house and I hid behind my new face."

The midmorning fog was starting to break up and the sun sent a bright ray into the front seat of the GTO. Grace moved her hand into its warming beam.

"I am miserable," she said with more truth than ever. "I need to confess to the police and I need to locate the family of the little girl"

"Do you know the girl's name?"

"Yes, I do. Her name was Robin Rose and I may have been related to her."

Thirty-Three

Come out, come out wherever you are
We're coming in our muscle car
Are you safe?
Are we?
Who will we see?
Wishing upon a star

~~~

*M*ichael appeared floored at the information that Grace gave him. It was such a long time ago. He must have assumed the mother of the little girl had moved on and put the tragedy behind her.

"What do you mean; you may have been related to her?"

"Well, it's just a hunch. I need to do a little more digging before I can say for sure."

Grace was not ready to share any more.

How disturbing this is for me, a family member? Wouldn't I have known if she was one of my own?

"How can I help?" Michael asked.

"Well, now that I have sat in it, and if you promise to go super slow, you could drive me."

"Of course! Where?"

"Muir Woods…home."

～

Grace pulled down BB's kitty food from the cupboard and put a scoop in his bowl. What a wonderful morning she'd had. For the first time in forty years, Grace did not feel alone. All of the guilt was still there, but like the ray of sun that warmed Michael's car seat, the truth was melting her cold resolve and Michael was willing to move forward with her.

Before she could turn herself in to the Marine County Sheriff's Department, Grace needed to search for something. *Yes, what was it exactly that I'm looking for? Each of these revelations and questions are like pieces to a puzzle.*

It was the memoir and poems that had started this thawing of her ridged existence. Even though she was famous and known around the globe, Grace lived a solitary existence, but as each poem and word flowed onto the page, the dark veil over her life began lifting.

One of the puzzle pieces was the gift her father had left her. Grace was sure it was the key to—not pardon—but peace. Her father was speaking to her from his own complicated grave. The Sidan words were his whispered verses, asking Grace for forgiveness. This was his way of offering something Grace always wanted—answers and perhaps, family.

Grace went back into the study to look for both.

TORMENT BLAND EDGE KNOWLEDGE FORGIVENESS STORM EARTHEN LOVE FEARLESS RUBY STRENGTH COASTAL FERAL TRAUMA KELP SPIRAL HOPE OCEAN AZURE SORRY FERN UNLOVED CHALLENGE CRAZY FAITH HEALING MISERY PEACE JUSTICE ROSE TRUST FROZEN SPAWNING WATERSHED HEIRLOOM DESPAIR DREAM MISUSE POLITICAL DEVINE EXPOSED HEAVEN

MERCY PINNACLE INSPIRE BLEED VALUE INTEGRITY TRAIL TIDAL WEALTH

Grace laid her hands on the tiles and moved them around randomly. Then she tucked them together so that the words read in rows. Three tiles were missing. GRACE, ROBIN, and one more that she could not recall. After studying the grouping for a few minutes, she stirred the pot once again and pulled out RUBY and ROSE. She looked at those two words and tried to come up with things that they had in common. They both started with the letter R. They both were beautiful gifts. They both had four letters. They both were names. She stepped back and looked again.

"I need to stack them like I did when I was ten," Grace said to BB, as if he understood her. She had him up on the desk and he was sitting patiently.

"Okay, here we go."

One by one Grace read aloud the word on each block before she placed it: OCEAN, FROZEN, CRAZY, TORMENT, TRAUMA, HOPE and on and on. As she picked up each tile she could feel her father's ghostly hand guiding each puzzle piece in place.

Which one is it? she asked in her mind. *What is the name of little Robin's twin?*

MISUSE, HEIRLOOM, FORGIVENESS, the Sidan stack got higher and more unstable.

It was all little BB could do, not to topple the whole thing.

Grace was nearing the top. She had only a few pieces to go, when it dawned on her. ROSE and RUBY were colors! That left two tiles to add to the tower: FERN and AZURE. Fern was a green color and azure was a bright, sky-blue. With a steady hand, Grace Ruby added her discovery.

She stepped back and looked at the solid stack of clues and felt something shift inside of her. She couldn't quite put her finger on it, but completing the tower felt like a start to a new life; not necessarily a better life, just a different one.

Grace wiggled her fingers at the base of the tower to catch BB's eyes. Then she moved her hand out of the way as her little kitty dove for the pretty pile of the clues, spilling them with a loud crash. Grace smiled as she watched him rustle around on top of the desk, scattering them every which way. Then she picked up FERN and AZURE and slipped the blocks of wood into the front pocket of her jeans, and went to get ready for her fist ride in a Pontiac GTO since 1966.

~

Grace gave Michael the address to the Sherriff's Department in Mill Valley. She buckled up and closed her eyes. Michel was quiet, drove slowly, and let her be.

Grace went over her theory in her mind. First was the eerie, unsettling, horrible connection to the words her father wrote on the Sidan blocks: her first and middle names, Grace Ruby, as well as the little girl that she had killed, Robin Rose.

Then there was the memory, which had floated to the top of her consciousness, of two little blonde girls sitting on the beach close to where Grace had spent her childhood. Grace herself had white blonde hair when she was little. Grace had the hopeful, yet sinking feeling that the girl she hit, had a twin, Grace's half-sister.

This was all just on coincidence and hunches. The first thing Grace needed to do, was go back to the box containing the evidence from the accident and see if there was a word or name on the block that was in her father's bomber jacket. Then she could use that name, along with either Fern or Azure as a middle name. For some reason, the police report did not give a last name of the deceased.

Grace's other sinking feeling was that the reason that there wasn't a last name was because of money, secrets, and covert affairs. Someone may have shut down the whole thing out of shame. This made Grace sad. In her heart, all she wanted to do now was confess, and hopefully apologize. That is if there was someone left to apologize to.

~

"Grace, open your eyes," Michael said as the quiet riding muscle car pulled onto the Golden Gate Bridge. Traffic was thick and the cars were barely moving.

Grace cracked open her eyes and looked at the view inside the car. Here she was sitting next to the man she had adored from afar. He truly was handsome, but it had nothing to do with his outward appearance. He had an inner light that seeped out of his skin. That light had drawn Grace to him, both when she was open and wild, and when she was closed and reserved.

"You know you were the hottest boy I had ever seen, back in 1966. But now, you take my breath away."

"Oh my, I just wanted you to see the ocean. It's such a beautiful day."

Grace turned and looked out at the bay side.

"Yes, it is a beautiful day, a beautiful day to set a story straight."

"About that, you don't have to set any record straight on my behalf," Michael's tone was serious.

"Oh, but I do. My whole life has been altered because of that lie. I honestly cannot take one more step forward until I make amends. Promise me that you will take care of BB if they arrest me."

"They're not going to arrest you. Is that why we're going to the Sherriff's Department?"

"Well, not at first. I need to retrieve something from the evidence box from our accident."

"I'm not sure you can do that," Michael added.

"Well, I just need to see it then."

"What is it?" Michael asked.

"A very important piece to the puzzle," Grace answered, as she closed her eyes once again.

~∾

"You're back," said the girl at the front desk. "What can I help you with today?"

Just as Grace was about to answer, Brad Heller poked his head out from the back room.

"Miss Van Vliet. Nice to see you again, did you forget something?"

"I need to see something in the evidence box again, something I may have missed."

"Oh, alright, who is this?"

"This is the other teen that was in the accident," Grace offered.

"Hello, I'm Michael Berkshire."

The two men shook hands as the three of them headed to the archive area.

"After you left, I read some more on your case. You were the driver of the car, weren't you?" Brad asked Michael.

Grace interrupted Michael before he could answer.

"I want to talk to someone about that, but first I need to check on something," Grace said while giving Michael a look of "let me do this my way".

As Brad rolled the ladder into place he said, "It's so strange. The deceased little girl's last name was not listed anywhere in the report. It's almost as if she was an orphan. The name ROBIN ROSE was found under her coat's tag, hand-written in ink. There's no record of a family."

"That's what we're trying to do; locate the family. We need to apologize," Michael said as Brad handed down the box.

"Back in those days, cases weren't covered as closely as today. Some things were just swept under the rug. How tragic for her, and for you as well," Brad said as he went back to his desk.

Michael sat the box on the floor. Grace stepped back to let him go through the contents alone. She could see painful memories coming to the surface from his body language. He lifted out Robin Rose's little coat and turned to Grace with tears in his eyes.

"Senseless, reckless," he whispered to her.

Grace nodded and held her arms out. Michael lowered the little white pea coat into the box and pulled Grace into an embrace. They stood that way, crying for a while, until Grace pulled away and reached in to retrieve the bomber jacket.

"Let's see if Robin Rose had a sister, okay?" Grace said quietly, as she put her hand in one pocket of the jacket and then the other. "Here it is."

Grace slowly pulled out the little Sidan puzzle piece. At first she saw only the blank side and was momentarily disappointed. But then she flipped the tile block over and read out loud, "RACHEL, her sister's name is Rachel!"

"How do you know? Are you sure?" Michael said, as he took the piece and looked at it himself.

"No, I'm not sure. But I believe Robin and Rachel were twins. Robin's middle name was Rose, and Rachel's middle name was either Fern or Azure."

Grace reached into her jeans pocket and pulled out the blocks with FERN and AZURE written on them. Michael took those pieces and looked at them.

"I don't understand," he said.

"Well, I think my father may have had another family that no one knew about, or maybe he had children with a mistress. I think Robin Rose and Rachel Fern or Azure are related to me, Grace Ruby. I believe we all had the same father.

"My father had all of our names written on these puzzle pieces that I grew up playing with. I think I killed my own sister!"

Grace was sobbing now and said that last sentence loud enough for Brad Heller to hear.

Michael pulled her into him even closer as Brad got out of his chair and headed back to the entwined couple standing over the evidence box.

"Excuse me, what did you say?" Brad was making his way down the narrow shelving rows.

"Yes, I need to tell you or maybe the district attorney. I have a confession to make."

"Grace no, no, you don't have to do this," Michael said, as she pulled away from him.

"Oh, I most certainly do."

"Let's step into the sheriff's office, shall we?" Brad had his arm behind Grace's back, guiding her back into the main part of the building. "Gretchen, get Jack in here please."

Brad left the two of them in a small office filled with family photos and accolades. Michael pulled out two chairs and offered one to Grace.

"You know, this is the moment I have been avoiding, sidestepping, fearing for forty-eight years." Grace sat down and stared at a framed certificate while she spoke. "I committed two of the most horrendous crimes imaginable, killing someone, and then lying about it. I built a life on wobbly ground, constantly watching over my shoulder to see if the fog of deceit would catch up to me. I forced everything to be calculated and perfect; for fear that just one tiny slip would bring everything tumbling down.

"I missed out on so much. I was vain and hurting before our accident, and I took that pain and spiraled down to a very dark place. I took you with me. There you were with your face rubbed off from the horrid windshield impact. I thought you were going to die or be a vegetable, but instead of being a 'big girl', I was an immature, 'little girl' and made the decision to lie. The lie wasn't an accident, it was a conscious, evil decision that I made next to your hospital bed.

"And now my desire to reveal myself has brought me to yet another tragic connection; that sweet little baby I hit, may have been my half-sister."

As Grace finished speaking, a big, burly man came into the office and shut the door.

"Hello, I'm Sheriff Anston. I understand you have something that you would like to say." His voice was deep and serious.

"Yes," Grace said as the sheriff sat behind his desk.

"Forty-eight years ago I committed a crime and lied about it. I would like to set the record straight and incur my much deserved penalty."

"I see," said the Sheriff. "May I record this without your lawyer present?"

"Yes."

"Wait Grace, maybe you should call your lawyer," Michael said. He was really trying to hold back.

"No, I'm ready," Grace stated firmly.

"Alright then," said Sheriff Anston as he pulled an old style recorder out of a desk drawer.

Grace then proceeded to tell her story.

When she was done, it was Michael's turn to speak up.

He told the sheriff that he had been drinking and that he had known that Grace was under the driving age when he let her get behind the wheel. He was perfectly content having the conviction on his record and on his shoulders all of these years.

"Give me a minute to review your case file," the sheriff said, as he pushed the pause button on the recorder and turned to his computer.

Grace and Michael waited patiently; both deep in thought.

"It says that you, Michael Berkshire, were initially charged with Gross Vehicular Manslaughter while intoxicated, but after the extent of your injuries were revealed, the charges were lowered and then dropped all together by the deceased's family.

"As for you, Miss Van Vliet, I am afraid your confession falls under the category of Statute of Limitations for Gross Vehicular Manslaughter. Had you come to us with this information within six years of the accident, you would have been able to right your wrong, but fortunately or unfortunately you are years too late.

"Let me ask you this; did you willfully with intention murder Robin Rose with the vehicle?"

"No, no, of course not!" Grace cried out.

"Well, I'm afraid you are going to have to make amends with the family of the deceased and perhaps within your own conscience.

"We will update the file, and log in your admission. What a horrible thing to live with all of these years. I hope you can find peace."

"May I keep this piece of evidence?" Grace asked while opening her clutched hand to reveal the puzzle block.

"Yes, but log that in with Brad."

With that Sheriff Anston showed them out of his office.

~~~

*M*ichael opened the exit door and the sun bathed both he and Grace with warmth. He reached down and took her hand as they headed to the car.

"What now?" he asked, as he opened the passenger door for her.

Grace reached in and pulled out the Sidan blocks from her pants pocket before getting into the car.

"I want to try and find my sister, but I don't know where to start."

"Well, let's go grab a bite to eat and talk it out. Surely, together we can put some memories and a few facts together."

Grace turned and looked at him with such feeling she thought her heart would burst.

"I've been alone for so long, and now you and my kitty gift are filling me up with…"

Grace looked down at the little pieces of wood in her hands. She couldn't finish her sentence and she loved that Michael didn't ask for more; he just started the car and drove.

~⁹

The Pontiac pulled into a parking space in downtown Mill Valley. Michael and Grace walked to Mama's Café and sat on a bench in the sun to wait for a table.

"I can't believe this place is still here," Michael said, as he looked down at the sample menu.

Grace was quiet. She was thinking about all that had just happened. The first thing that came to her was how the world just kept rolling along; nothing stopped, no earth shattering quake. Here she sat, minutes after confessing to her crimes, and people were having lunch and taking walks as if nothing had happened. All of the 'holding on to control', all of the precise living, all of the jaw clenching constraint...none of it changed anything. The little girl was long dead; there was nothing she could do to bring her back.

She wasn't even sure she felt differently after letting the police know the truth. The sheriff was right; she was going to have to find what she was searching for in the face of the stricken.

The hope was that the tête-a-tête to poor Robin, her twin Rachel, would be willing and/or able to meet me, the villain, Grace Ruby.

A waitress led them to a table, and brought them waters. "You know, little girl, I always assumed that I was Kid Flash. Oh yes, I was that super hero that could go beyond the speed of light and move around the globe in the blink of an eye. That's why I wanted to join the air force and fly fighter jets. I wanted to go as far away from home as possible, as fast as possible.

"But then I met you. After our kiss, I began to have second thoughts about enlisting. That's why I started drinking in the car.

I wanted to sabotage my attempt at joining by going in drunk, just so I could stay home and date you!"

The waitress returned and placed their food on the table. Both Michael and Grace had ordered oversized omelets filled with vegetables and cheese.

"For the first time in my life, I wanted to go slow," he continued.

Grace buttered Michael's toast and offered it to him.

"But then time decelerated to a sickening halt while I recovered in the hospital. I kept picturing you moving on with the real Kid Flash. I knew that you wouldn't want me when you saw my face. I slipped further and further into depression.

"Then one day, I learned that all of my enlisted recruit buddies were killed in a plane crash on their way overseas. I was scheduled to be on that same plane. My first thought was, 'That little girl, Grace Ruby saved me...she saved my life.'"

Grace inhaled sharply as he finished that last sentence.

What me? I saved a life?

"But, at what expense; a life for a life?" Grace asked.

"The world is mysterious and wonderful, awful and amazing all at once," Michael said.

It was his turn to butter her bread. He added fresh strawberry jam.

"Sometimes someone is in the right place at the right time, even if it seems horribly wrong. Sometimes there is a bigger picture that only God understands. Everything happens for a reason. I truly believe that, little girl. Truly I do."

"Excuse me," the waitress was back and stood between the couple. "Do I know you?" She was looking at Grace.

Oh dear, everywhere I go this happens.

"Yes, I am 'that' author," Grace said kindly.

"No, no, you just look like someone that comes in here every once and awhile," said the young woman as she topped off both coffees.

"Really?" Michael piped up.

"Yes, but her hair is much lighter than yours. You have the same shaped face and eyes. You could be twins," the girl exclaimed as she turned to go to another table.

"See, being at the right place at the right time," Michael said as he leaned in towards Grace and touched the side of her cheek with his hand. "Let's ask her what else she knows about this other beautiful woman when she comes back. Shall we?"

What is this man doing to me? All these years I thought I was the person that caused horrible, bad things to happen to people. So I locked myself up in my Sidan tower and threw away my joy key. And now, this man is pulling out my sadness block by block, just by being supportive and kind, and 'there'! My perfectly solid life is starting to fall apart in a subtle, wonderful way.

Grace leaned back in her seat and reached into her pocket to pull out her sister's first and middle name choices. She aligned the three little blocks with the words facing the edge of the table while Michael flagged their young waitress down with his famous salute and tiny wave. Grace was feeling hopeful that Michael was right about the world being both mysterious, and wonderful.

RACHEL FERN AZURE

"Hello, yes, we were just wondering if you know the name of the lady that you say looks like me. Do any of these names look familiar?"

Grace pointed down at the little blocks on the table.

"Hmm," the waitress paused, "let me go get Gina. She usually works the morning shift. Maybe she knows."

Grace took a bite of the jellied toast and washed it down with coffee. The combination of butter, bread, strawberries, cream, and coffee was exquisite.

"Well I'll be. You look just like Azi," said a woman about Grace's age with a manager's coat on.

"Azi, as in Azure?" Grace asked as her jaw dropped.

"Why yes."

"Wow, really?" said Michael. "Do you happen to know where she lives?"

"Yes I do. We were just talking about that the other day. She lives up on Muir Woods Road, in one of the cottages.

Grace dropped the piece of toast she was holding onto her plate. A small amount of blood red jam spattered across the white tablecloth.

"Oh dear, just a minute, I'll clean that for you," Gina said, as she left to retrieve something.

"Did she just say Muir Woods Road? That's the road that I used to live on."

Grace was shaking now. She hadn't been back there for four decades.

"Didn't you live in one of the cottages there, too?" Grace asked Michael, as she tried to dab at the red stain with her napkin.

"Yes, before the accident. After, my family moved into the city to be closer to UCSF for my surgeries. This is exciting Grace. We know where she lives and we know her name."

"Yes," Grace said with trepidation, "I have a sister and her name is Rachel Azure."

"But what is her last name? Is it the same as yours?" Michael asked.

"I don't think so. Surely that would have come out at some time," Grace answered. "When I was ten years old, my father was killed in a car accident not far from our accident spot. Later I found out that a woman was in the car with him and was killed as well. I'm wondering if that was the mother of the twins."

"Do you know her name?"

"Looks like we need to go back to the Sheriff's office and check," Michael said as he signaled for the check.

"Hi Gretchen, we're back," Michael said while leaning onto the high counter. "Is Mr. Heller still available?"

"I'll check, just a moment."

"This time we are looking for the name of the deceased female passenger from a fatal accident involving my father," Grace said. She sat down in the chair next to Brad's desk and computer.

"Oh my, you have had your share of tragedy. Can you tell me the date?"

"Let's see, I was ten, so that would have been 1962. I believe it was late summer or early fall. I actually saw the accident."

"You did? Oh my, how horrible. Where was it? Where were you?" Michael clutched Grace's arm and shoulder and squatted down next to her.

"I was standing at Overlook Cliff. I had just come up from clam digging. A storm developed quickly and I was angry that I needed to go home. I heard a horrible noise and then I saw my father's red sports car sail off the cliff and crash on the rocks below. Later I learned that my father was having an affair with the woman that died with him."

"Oh my God," Michael said while blinking away tears.

"My father's name was John Van Vliet," Grace said to both men.

"Here it is," Brad said, as he turned the computer screen so that Grace and Michael could read it.

DOUBLE FATALITY. ONE MALE. ONE FEMALE. CAR ACCIDENT. NO FAULT.
John Van Vliet, driver. Carol Zurig, passenger. Sept. 27, 1966.

"Could my sister's name be Rachel Azure Zurig? Can you look that up somewhere please?"

"It says here that Carol Zurig had no children. She was an employee of Merck and Company, and is listed as single," Brad read from the screen.

"That's the company my father worked for," Grace said, as she turned towards Michael.

"Can you think of anyone else?"

And then it hit her, Grace slid back out of the room into her memory. She was ten again and in pain. Her father had just been buried and she was sulking on the front porch of her family's cottage home. In her arms she held her big, orange cat. She was pulling her fingers through his fur, listening to her mother and Auntie Mae argue. Grace could smell gin and limes, and hear glasses clinking with ice.

"And what about Jennifer Hexel, remember her?" Grace could hear her aunt's slurred words as clear as day.

Jennifer Hexel? Who was Jennifer Hexel? Grace remembered wondering.

"Is there someone living on Muir Woods Road named Rachel Azure Hexel, or maybe Azi Hexel?" Grace asked Brad. But before he could answer, Grace knew she was right. She could feel it in her heart and in her bones.

"Yes, I have an Azi Hexel and here's her address."

"We found her," cried Michael. And Grace felt the omelet in her stomach turn towards the beach.

Thirty-Four

Grace, sweet grace is always inside us
Resting quietly until needed
To have it and hold it is a gift
Precious and eternal

But to give grace to others
Is a building block beyond human failings
Moving the soul closer to God
In unimaginable, wondrous ways

"Let's not go just yet," Grace said as she and Michael got back into the car. "Take me for a drive. Let's go up Highway One, I need to face my fears."

"Wow, are you sure?"

"As long as you are at the wheel, I'll be fine," Grace answered, as she pushed the button to roll down her window.

The Marin County afternoon was gorgeous. The sky overhead was a deep, rich azure blue. Late spring blooms were visible from the road and contrasted against the green of the forest.

Grace grabbed gulps of ocean air as Michael came up to the first vista point. With each breath she could feel herself unwinding.

"Oh my, the ocean looks so different here than in the city. It looks fresh and alive and exciting!"

Michael edged the GTO faster. Grace grabbed onto the arm rest and he slowed back down.

"Easy now, break me in slowly," Grace teased.

"Okay little girl. I forget that we're at an advanced age."

Michael turned the radio on to an oldies station, and the two of them fell quiet as they listened to the words and music of their youth.

The big muscle car glided easily around the hairpin turns of Highway One. Grace closed her eyes when they passed the spot of their accident and then opened them to see more beautiful vistas and white gulls soaring over the cliffs along the road. Gradually, Grace loosened her grip on the armrest and relaxed into the rhythm of a drive with her handsome neighbor. It was so soothing driving away from what she needed to do. But soon the car would be turning around, and Grace and Michael would be heading back to face the music.

Paperback writer, paperback writer!

"When you get to Stinson Beach, let's turn around. I think I'm ready."

"Whatever happens," Michael said, as he pulled in to a turnabout, "I just want to make sure that Azi knows that this is not just about you. I want her to know that I am equally responsible. She may take our news badly. She may be angry, afraid, or not want to speak to us at all. No matter what happens, my darling Grace, I will be by your side today and for as long as you will have me."

Grace reached over and put her hand on Michael's thigh. She turned her head away, toward the ocean and let grateful, happy tears roll down her face.

Is this what love feels like?

Grace had really never had a healthy, working relationship model to look at. She felt her parents loved her, but now she realized that they could not have loved each other; *why else would my father have affairs and start a family with another woman? Maybe my own mother was "the other woman" to some other poor lady? Maybe my family was the illegitimate one?*

Oh, it's all so confusing, Grace thought as the sun shone brightly across the expanse of blue. *Maybe Rachel Azure Hexel will have the answers. Maybe my little sister, Azi will have the last pieces to the Sidan puzzle.*

~⁹

Grace gave directions to her growing up home. It was three roads down from where Michael's family lived. They pulled up and Grace was flooded with wonderful memories. The structure of the cottage was still the same, but everything had been refaced and updated. She could see her old bedroom window from the angle they were parked; the window that she would sneak out of to head to the woods to explore or escape. There was the front porch, painted now in a bright white, and the original front door with its dark green hinges.

Here is where so many wonderful things happened before she was ten. In her mind she could see herself setting up the Sidan game to lure her father over to play with her. She could smell her mother cooking something amazing for dinner, and hear the television droning out theme songs from their favorite shows.

Then sadness came over Grace. She began to recall all of the days and nights that her father was away. She could hear her mother's quiet crying late in the night, after Grace went to bed. Then the pain of not having a father at all, having him gone forever; followed by the realization that he had not been faithful to either her mother or to Grace.

Lastly, Grace felt the horrible, horrible guilt of not being there for her dear, sweet mother. *What a selfish girl I was; so caught up in my own pain. It was almost as if it was too much to bear. I felt that if I stopped for one moment to comfort my mother, both of us would have disappeared from earth. She was there for my living, but I left her while she was dying.*

"Grace, look," Michael said, startling Grace from her thoughts.

Two little boys were crawling out of Grace's old bedroom window. They dropped to the ground, grabbed a couple of buckets and ran into the thicket that led to Grace's old hidden path. Their buckets were a bright, bright orange.

"That's my secret trail. That's the gateway to my escape." Grace was sitting up straight, peering out the GTO's windshield.

"Well, what are you waiting for? Get out, get going, I'll drive up to my old house and wait for you there."

"What? Oh, maybe. Well, okay." Grace put her hand on the door release, then turned and looked at Michael. He smiled and nodded encouragement. Grace broke out in a radiant, gigantic smile in return; a smile that broke through her sixty-two years and revealed her inner child.

"I won't be long," Grace said, as she opened the car door and hurried to the opening in the undergrowth.

~

*O*h *the glorious smells of nature,* Grace thought, as she ducked down and pushed her way into the bowels of the woods. Wet, moist, alive, earthy, rich, acrid…the scents threw her back in time. She inhaled and felt her whole body relax and rejuvenate.

Grace stood still and looked down at the debris on the forest floor; tiny bits of the giant redwoods, skin cells that had flaked off over the millennium.

There was a lesson here. Grace stepped closer to the trunk of one of her towering tree brothers. She laid her hands on the rough bark and felt silent words come to her.

We are whole. We are stronger than we know. Life often robs us of bits of ourselves, but those pieces do not fall far from the source. We have roots, we have substance, and we give to the world just by existing. We also have flaws and troubles that shape us. Those tribulations often make us stronger. Most importantly we are never truly in control. Our job is to recover, learn, and receive the lesson without steering the ship. Let go, dear Grace, let go.

Grace lifted her hands away and tipped her head back. She could see a bit of blue sky through the thick branches.

"Alright, my wise brothers," Grace whispered, "I will try and move on."

With that, Grace took a small step down the path to forgiving herself. As Grace Ruby pushed through the undergrowth and wound her way through the ferns and tree trunks, she began shedding her controlling prison. No matter what was going to happen with her sister, she was going to loosen her rigid ways and begin to live once again. Confession may not change a thing, but it can be freeing and Grace was slowly letting that realization untie her binds.

She left her path and started heading up the road where she first met Michael so very long ago. His family's cottage had a long, steep driveway. Some of the older trees had been removed, but Grace could see that younger ones were popping up as replacements.

As she rounded the last turn she saw him. Michael was leaning casually on the back of his new Pontiac with his legs crossed at the ankles and his hands in his pockets. He stood up and gave his little salute wave when he saw Grace hiking up the drive.

"Hey little girl, what took you so long?" Michael called out to Grace.

"I like to keep a guy waiting," Grace answered.

"Well, did it have to be for forty-eight years?" Michael quipped and they both laughed a deep and loving laugh.

"I'm nervous about meeting Rachel, but at the same time I'm ready to apologize and move forward."

"Come here, little girl," Michael said as he pulled Grace to the side of the car. "You have nothing to be nervous about. I'll be right there with you."

Grace put her back against the passenger door and Michael leaned into her. He pressed both hands against the sides of Grace's face.

"You are an amazing, talented, beautiful woman. We've both spent many years apart. I had an amazing wife and career, and have two beautiful children. You were and are a bestselling author known around the world. But now is now, and for the years that I have left on this planet, well, I would love to spend them with you."

Michael then pushed his lips on hers and kissed her with such unrestrained passion that Grace's knees started to buckle. She was fourteen all over again. The gray hair, the wrinkles, none of that mattered; a kiss was a kiss, and a great kiss was unforgettable.

"I would love that too," Grace whispered as she pulled back and looked into his blue eyes. "I'm so humbled that you're willing to give me a fresh start."

She reached up and wrapped her arms around him and squeezed him tight. In that moment, she never, ever wanted to let him slip away again.

"Let's go see if I have any family left that I can introduce you to. I'm going to need you by my side as I speak the truth. My heart is ready to reveal," Grace said after a second long, deep kiss.

Grace Ruby and Michael Berkshire got into their muscle car and drove down the curvy road towards the ocean, as a little bit of fog started to form over the treetops.

Thirty-Five

Art heals, reveals, lifts the spirit
Invisible connection to source
Expression, emotion stuns the heart
And moves both artist and audience
To deeper understanding

~⟩

*M*y *church*, thought Grace as Michael wound the powerful car though the cathedral of redwoods. How safe and at peace Grace felt cradled in the arms of her brothers. Red alders, big leaf maples, tanoaks, and Douglas firs; all sitting at the feet of eight-hundred year old giants waiting for the day's sermon. Sunday after Sunday, Grace had moved from one house of worship to another, searching for a place to hide her conscience. She had entered into each space without an open heart and, by being closed at all times, Grace could not receive.

But her brothers were speaking to her now. *Where have you been? Come home. Come back to your true self. Breathe the fresh air. Dig your heels into the sand alongside Mother Ocean. Allow grace to flow through you.* Grace was listening and hearing, even though the language was not English, the message was clear and Grace received.

~⟩

"What's the address again?" Michael asked, as he slowed the car down. "Oh, this must be it."

Grace braced herself. She hadn't even rehearsed what she was going to say.

"Wow, this place is amazing." Michael said, as he pulled off to the side at the base of the steep driveway.

A lit sign hung from a tree branch:

AZI'S ART STUDIO
11:00A.M.-10:00P.M.
Tues-Fri

"She's an artist," Grace whispered, "like you!"

"Oh, I just dabble."

They both got out of the car at the same time.

"Look at all the Christmas lights strung up into the redwoods. How in the world did someone do that?" Michael was looking up as he hit the car lock on his fob.

"Let's walk, okay?" Grace said.

The sun was setting and the misty fog a perfect backdrop for the hundreds of tiny pinpoints of light lining the path. Whimsical sculptures were strategically placed among the ferns and sorrel. Grace saw strange rabbits and bulbous-nosed gnomes. Michael pointed out a long, thin dragon wound around a Douglas fir. The art was clean and colorful. Nothing was cluttered or overdone. It was like experiencing a walk of discovery; each bend in the path brought a new delight.

"What are we going to say to her?" Grace finally broached the subject as they strolled.

"Well, let's make sure she is who we think she is, before we spring the past on her."

"Good idea," Grace Ruby said, as she threaded her arm into Michael's.

"Then we're going to have to play it by ear," Michael added.

Grace got quiet and took stock of her feelings. When she first ventured into writing her memoir, she had no intention of seeking forgiveness, resolution, or comfort. Her desire was to tell her story and finally release her lies. She in no way thought that speaking the truth would have led to all of this: a kitten, Michael, and now maybe a sister.

What if it all goes horribly wrong? Normally, controlled Grace would not be putting herself in this type of situation. *I would be having a cup of tea, locked safely in my tower.*

She was in a different environment now, with a man on her arm, and an armor of truth protecting her from harm. Her tree brothers, quiet as always, were lit up like the Milky Way. They seemed to be pointing her in the right direction. Grace slipped off her introverted costume and let her ten year old extroverted self return, as she and Michael approached the charming cottage studio.

"Hello," Michael called quietly.

The studio door was propped open with an easel.

Just as Grace was about to lift her foot to the first step of the porch, panic and anxiety hit her like a car. She froze. Her heart pounded and sweat broke out on her chest and forehead.

"What is it, Grace?" Michael stepped back down to the ground level with her.

"I, I don't know. I can't breathe. What am I doing here?"

Michael turned her around and gently had her sit on the steps.

"Here we are," Grace said in a panicked, soft whisper, "about to go into a stranger's place of business and announce that I am her sister's murderer. How horrible, how awful to turn a person's life upside down...just so I can get things off my chest? I can't, I can't do it!"

"Okay, okay then let's go. Both you and I have had a very eventful day. Let's go back to the city and take things slower."

Grace pulled long, slow breaths into her lungs. She closed her eyes and tried to picture putting things off for yet, another day.

"Wait, just wait, let me sit for a minute."

Michael draped his arm around her and pulled her to him. Grace's heart slowed and her shoulders relaxed.

"Okay, I'm better now, but this has to go gently. I don't want to do this woman harm as well."

"Yes, soft and sweet, like you. Let's just meet the artist and take it from there. Alright?"

"Yes, yes of course," Grace let Michael help her up. Out of habit she slipped her hands into her pants pockets.

What is this? Oh yes, the Sidan blocks with the names Rachel and Azure. Grace had left the block with the word Fern on it back in the car. The last two blocks that were missing were the ones with the names Robin and Grace on them. She put Azure back in her pocket and kept Rachel in her hand. In her mind she felt her father's ghostly fingers brush over hers and steady her grip.

"Let's go in. I'm ready."

Michael stepped in first with Grace behind him. The wooden floor creaked as their weight announced their arrival.

"Oh my," was all Michael got out.

Grace Ruby moved beside him and was stunned.

The first things she saw were soaring sculptures of Sidan towers reaching up to the vaulted ceilings of the studio. Each stack was glued in a way to represent motion. Some had blocks being pulled out or pushed in. Others were leaning precariously over the center of the room. The towers reminded Grace of the surrounding giant coastal redwoods. They seemed to be guarding the space. The lighting was amazing. Different colors were tucked into the centers of the stacks and each tower glowed ruby, rose, or blue.

Grace gasped a breath when she moved in closer to the art on the walls.

Among fantastic, surrealistic acrylic paintings of Muir Woods, there were delicate pen and ink drawings of twins in dozens of poses. The black and white silhouettes were subtle contrasts to the brightly colored, larger framed pieces.

"Look Michael, look at this," Grace spoke with reverence.

He pulled himself away from a sculpture of a tiny girl sitting crossed legged on a rock made from wire.

"That must be them; she has captured her memories and put them on paper," whispered Grace. "And look at this one."

Grace had moved to a larger work done with pastels. Two little blonde babies were propped up on an orange blanket on the beach.

Michael and Grace moved in closer.

"Is that me?" said Grace.

Standing off to the side of the babies was a girl around four or five years old with long, skinny legs and long blonde hair blowing off her shoulders.

"Did I have a relationship with these girls?"

Grace backed up and almost stumbled as she heard, "Ahem, well I'll be. I've been waiting for you, dear sister, for a million and a half years."

Both Grace and Michael turned around. There stood a petite woman in a long flowing dress. Over the dress was an apron with paint splattered across. The woman had snow white hair and she wore flip-flops on her feet. She smiled warmly and opened her arms.

"How I've missed you, sweet sister," the woman said.

"Are you Rachel Azure Hexel?" Michael asked, as Grace slowly staggered forward.

"Yes, but please call me Azi. I haven't gone by Rachel for years."

Stunned, Grace moved towards Azi's open arms like a zombie. She couldn't take her eyes off the angelic face before her.

"Come on. It's alright." Azi coaxed Grace into the space between her open arms.

Finally she made it and the shorter woman embraced her affectionately.

"You are still so beautiful," Azi said to Grace.

"Do you know me?" Grace asked as she stepped back and opened her hand to show Azi the Sidan block with the word RACHEL printed on it.

"Oh, my there's the other one! Come over here."

Azi took Grace's hand and pulled her over to a different art wall. There, mounted in a darkly stained redwood frame, were two little Sidan pieces with the names ROBIN and GRACE printed on them.

Grace couldn't believe it. She was still in shock. She held the RACHEL block up by the others.

"Together, once again," sang out Azi. "Come on let's go into the house. I'll make some coffee and we can talk. And you are?"

"Michael, Michael Berkshire." The words tumbled from his mouth.

"Oh yes. It was your car, wasn't it? Come on now. Don't be shy. Do you like cream, or do you take yours black?"

Grace and Michael turned and looked at each other, dumbfounded, and then followed the tiny angel through the back of the studio.

～⁹

Azi's cottage home was attached to the studio by a tin roofed, open breezeway. The forest bumped right up to the edges of the walkway. Grace reached out her hand and let the fronds of the bordering ferns run through her fingers as they walked.

Michael was making small talk, but Grace's mind was racing.

Is this woman my full blooded sister? Did my mother have twins that she gave away? She seems to know about me. Maybe she's just a fan. Maybe she's read my bios on my books.

"Grace. Grace," Michael called. "What time did we get here this morning?"

"Eleven, I think."

Azi led them into the home. Grace felt warm, immediately. The A-roof beams, done in a yellow maple, were beautifully bare. West facing, floor to ceiling windows looked out into the lit forest. In the center of the room a huge, geometrically pattered rug anchored the space. On the rug, four oversized chairs faced a waist high glass table covered with books and magazines. The kitchen was all part of the same, inviting open space.

Azi took coffee beans from the freezer.

"Sit down, sit down please," she said, as she whirred the beans in a grinder.

Michael took Grace's hand and guided her to the chair facing the kitchen. He squeezed her hand firmly and then sat facing the window.

"I have so many questions," Azi called out as she ran water into the coffee urn.

Michael laughed loudly. "Not as many as we have for you!" He looked at Grace and gave her an encouraging nod.

Grace was clutching the armrests, trying to get all of her ducks in a row.

"Let's see," Azi said, as she brought over a creamer and sugar set. Grace recognized it as her grandmother's pattern. The same pattern as the teacup she had dropped in the sink.

"So, you don't remember me?" she asked Grace.

The coffee pot beeped and Azi filled three mugs and made two trips to the chairs.

"Thank you," Grace said as she accepted the steaming mug. The coffee smelled delicious. Grace reached down and poured in some cream to cool it.

"Not really. I have a vague memory of seeing you two little girls sitting on a beach blanket."

"You don't remember playing Sidan with us or digging for clams?"

Grace shook her head no. She still couldn't even believe she was talking with this woman. Grace pinched her arm and took a sip of coffee.

"Daddy really did a number on you, didn't he?"

Grace looked at Michael and he appeared enthralled. He was cradling his mug with both hands up by his chest.

"And mother," Azi continued, "was devastated when he took you away."

Azi leapt up from her chair to refill the creamer.

Grace's mind was spinning. *Took me away? What did she mean by that?*

Azi came back and sat Indian style in her chair.

"Every time he would take you back after sneaking you over for a bit, our mother would just go crazy."

"Are you saying that Jennifer Hexel was my mother?"

"Yes!" Azi said.

Grace closed her eyes, tears rolled down her checks. She had come fully expecting to shock and horrify Rachel Azure with her admission of guilt. But it was Azi's turn to pull out a precariously placed Sidan block.

"You mean the woman that raised me was not my mother?"

"Oh dear, no. She is the woman that our father ran off with and took you with him."

"I, I don't understand." Grace was sobbing now. Michael got up and went to look for tissue.

"There's some in the washroom," Azi told Michael, as she pointed to a hallway.

"You see," Azi continued, "we were illegitimate. Daddy never married our mother."

"But why not?" Grace blew her nose on the tissue and watched Michael sit back down.

"Because our mother was from the wrong side of the tracks! Grandmother would have nothing to do with her. So she forced

Daddy to marry a girl that fit the social standing of his heritage. Shortly after Robin and I were born, he took up with Ava. But Ava couldn't have children and our mother had her hands full with us, so he took you to live with them."

"I don't remember any of this."

"Neither do I, but in later years Mom explained it all to me. Everyone, including Grandmother, brain washed you into thinking Ava was your mother.

"Things were different back then," Azi continued. "If you didn't have status or money, you weren't included in the wealthy world. Grandmother threatened to pull all rights away from Daddy if he stayed with us, so he left. Because of that, he was able to secretly send our mother money to live on.

"Over the years, Daddy would sneak over to be with us. That, I do remember and sometimes he would bring you."

"How awful. How could he separate us like that?" Grace asked.

"I don't know. Money, I guess. I do know that he loved all of us very much. My twin and I were six when he passed."

Grace's mind was reeling. She excused herself and went to the washroom.

This was all such a mystery, a mystery that also explained a lot.

Grace had always wondered why she never really, truly felt a deep love for her mother. There never seemed to be a connection. Oh, she treasured the woman. She was sweet and kind, but she was also distant. And those nights when her father left Grace alone with her mother seemed to be tortuous for both of them. Ava must have known that father's heart was with Jennifer.

A thought came to Grace. *Maybe the woman in the car that was killed with Father really was just his secretary. Maybe they WERE just heading into work. Could it be that Father wasn't the philandering horrible person we believed him to be? Was he just stuck holding both sides of his own Sidan tower upright?*

Grace splashed water on her face and went back in to hear more.

"I was a witness to our father's car crash," Grace said as she took her place facing the kitchen.

"What? I didn't know that," Azi sat up straighter in her chair. "What happened?"

"I was ten and I was coming up from a clam dig. A storm blew in quickly and he must have been driving too fast for the slick highway. His car flew right over my head. Somehow, in that instant I knew it was him. But instead of climbing down the embankment to see if I could help, I ran away. I have carried that guilt with me for fifty-two years."

"Oh Grace, you were just a little girl. That's what little girls are supposed to do; how horrible. We were in Mrs. Piedmont's first grade class, when Mom came to take us home and tell us. I remember being sad, but by then, he really wasn't a part of our day to day.

"In later years, Mother told me that she had been so worried that the money would stop coming in after Father's passing, that she made a trip to San Francisco to talk to Grandmother Van Vliet. Grandmother said that our father had set up a trust for my mother and for us. She said in order for that trust to be honored, we were never to speak to you or see you again."

Michael got up to refill the mugs. Both women were silent as everything settled in.

"Were you living near Grace at the time?" Michael asked to break the tension in the room.

"Closer to Mill Valley," Azi answered. "After the accident, we moved to the cottage closest to Redwood Creek; the little cabin near Muir Beach."

Grace got up from her chair and walked over to the huge window facing the thickest parts of the forest.

"Tell me about Robin Rose." Grace's voice was faint and shaking with emotion. "What was little Robin like?"

"Robin was the athlete and the adventurer. She could never sit still. I loved to stay indoors and color and she liked to climb trees and build forts. She was an insomniac. She survived on very little sleep. We would wake to hear her pounding nails in our treehouse at one in the morning, or find her lining up the Sidan game on the patio railing like dominos; tipping the lead block and watching the pieces tumble onto each other, one at a time.

"She hated school and longed to be a sailor or an arctic explorer. She was always going off on adventures and Mother would worry and worry until she came home. Our teachers often said she was unruly and lacked focus. They would compare her to me and expect us to act as identical as we looked. Robin did not like that—she wanted to be her own person. I would wear dresses and she would wear denim pants. I would braid and plaster my hair in place. Robin would let hers go unruly and natural...like her personality."

"Did you two ever talk about me?" Grace didn't like the sound of the question as soon as she said it, but she really did want to know.

"Oh yes. We pictured you as a princess living in a castle with a moat around it. And when we were really little, we thought you were our fairy godmother, because you would come and play dolls and games with us and then leave."

Grace got more tissue and went back and sat down. She sipped some coffee and thought, *Not a princess or fairy godmother, more like anyone's worst nightmare; more like the Grim Reaper.*

She steadied her heart to tell the truth, noticing that the coffee was ice cold now.

Thirty-Six

"Amazing Grace, how sweet the sound,
That saved a wretch like me.
I once was lost but now am found,
Was blind, but now I see.

Through many dangers, toils and snares
I have already come;
'Tis Grace that brought me safe thus far
And Grace will lead me home."

John Newton

~~~

Grace scooted to the edge of her chair.
"I notice you have a lit path leading west. Does that run down to the ocean?" Grace asked.

"Yes and the state has solar lights overhead beyond my property."

"Well, do you mind if we go for a walk? I could use some fresh evening air," Grace said as she looked at Michael.

"Grace and I would like to share with you what happened the night Robin passed," Michael said as he stood up and gathered the empty mugs to take into the kitchen.

"Oh, of course. Can I get you a sweater, Grace?"

"Please, it may get chilly."

Azi got up and went into the back. Grace went to the kitchen area.

"I'm so nervous," Grace said to Michael quietly.

"So am I. But the truth is all we have."

"Here you go," Azi called out.

Grace's heart soared. The hoodie sweater was orange, a warm cozy orange.

~~~

The night time forest air outside of Azi's home took on a whole different persona; no longer dry and filled with filtered sunlight, the exhalations of the giant trees blew moist, cool air up from the Pacific.

Grace, Michael, and Azi began the downhill trek in a line, with Michael leading the way. Everyone was breathing in the living air.

"I'm not sure if you know this or not, but it was my car that hit your twin sister and killed her," Michael stated boldly not far into their hike.

"Yes, I knew that," Azi answered. Her voice wasn't as strong as it was in the house.

"I was getting ready to enlist in the air force and I wanted one last night of free fun. I had just met Grace that afternoon and invited her to go for a midnight drive." Grace slowed up a bit, to let Michael speak what was on his heart.

Grace was at the back of the hiking line. With each step she felt more like her old self, even through the tough conversation. The giant ferns, the springy bark underfoot; all of it was seeping into her bones like dark tea water.

Michael continued, "But then Grace gave me a kiss, and it changed me. In that instant I wanted my life to go in a whole different direction. So...we turned the car around and I started drinking. I wanted to have alcohol in my bloodstream so that they wouldn't accept me at the recruiter's office the next morning."

Graced hurried forward to interrupt Michael.

"Here it is. Azi, hold on a second." The little group exited the path and stopped at Look Out Point.

Grace turned Azi towards her and took both of her hands. The misty fog was lightly covering the moon and stars.

"Michael was not driving the car back that night, I was; it was me. I killed our sister! I was fourteen, suicidal, wild, crazed, reckless and I lied about the whole thing. I told the police that Michael had been drinking and driving and had hit a deer. But it wasn't Michael, and it wasn't a deer. It was a beautiful spirit floating across the highway in the fog.

"The woman that I thought was my mother was dying of cancer. I had been placed in a horrible boarding school. I thought my deceased father to be an adulterer. I was a wreck. I didn't want to live. I was going to drop Michael off and accelerate right off this very point; the same point that our father lost his life.

"The death of that precious baby altered everything. I didn't get the opportunity to end my own life that night. Instead I ran over a little girl and maimed the boy of my dreams. I took her beautiful life but she saved my retched one. I myself was free from physical harm and allowed to live, so I built the rest of my life on a tedious tower of controlled lies. I stopped feeling sorry for myself and I just existed. I was a slayer and a liar, and my soul died that horrible night.

"And now, years later, I find out the child was my own sister, our sister, a sister that I didn't even know that I had!"

Grace was sobbing and could barely get out the last few words. Her throat had closed up with the bitterness of all of her pent up emotions. She cracked her eyes open to see Rachel Azure's reaction and held a bit of fog in her lungs.

When the tear water cleared, Grace couldn't believe her eyes. There before her, was her younger sister staring up at her with such love and compassion, Grace's knees buckled and she collapsed to the sandy ground. Azi did not let go of Grace's hands, and she too went down. Michael rushed over to the women, but the two just released their grip and offered one hand each to Michael so that he could join them. The tall, lanky sixty-six year old, gingerly took each woman's hand and sat down upon the earth.

The three of them formed a circle of a tragic past. They sat on the cliff high above the Pacific in silence. Each person was clutching each hand with such fierceness, words were not necessary.

Grace looked over at Michael and saw, for an instant, the speed loving boy of eighteen. She could see the anguish beneath the skin of his reconstructed appearance. Grace watched Michael as he turned his head to look at Azi. Everything was moving in slow motion. As soon as his eyes alit on Azi's face, a transformation happened. Grace could see tension and guilt, falling from his features.

What am I witnessing?

Grace could feel Azi giving her a deeper squeeze with her hand. She brought her attention back to her younger sister.

Rachel Azure smiled and Grace felt something so deep inside of her that it took her a moment to realize what it was.

It was grace. Azi was offering Grace Ruby, unconditional, unmerited, pure grace. Not forgiveness, not restitution…but grace.

A stiff breeze came up and Grace lifted her head to see that a wispy bit of fog had blown away and a few stars were visible. Grace remembered following the little girl, her sister Robin, that night and hearing her hum the melody to *When You Wish Upon a Star*.

The end of her memoir came to Grace Ruby as one last poem…

> *Out of the blue,*
> *Grace comes into view.*
> *When you least expect it*
> *Your dreams can come true.*

Grace Ruby then opened her heart and received her sister's offering.

Epilogue

Family
Pure and simple
Sweet icing
Smoothing over life's rough patches
To take the sting out of tribulations
With a heavenly taste
Of
Grace

From the Rachel and Robin series

⁓

"Grammy Grace, Grammy Grace, I can't do it," little Rosy J called up from the beach. The tiny five-year-old had curly red hair like her mother, Michael's daughter.

"Tap the ground with your shovel like Grammy showed you. The clams will blow bubbles at you," Grace called down from her spot on the porch overhang.

"Okay, loves you lots," Rosy J sang out while looking down at the sand.

The whole family was visiting for the weekend. Michael's son with his new wife, Alice came up from L.A. Michael's daughter and son-in-law, along with Rosy J and another baby on the way came over from Napa. And Grace's little sister, Auntie Azi, still lived in her artist's cottage in Mill Valley.

Both Michael and Grace had sold their San Francisco properties and together bought a modern, four bedroom home overlooking Schoolhouse Beach just north of Bodega Bay.

"More coffee?" Michael asked as he came out onto the porch holding the pot.

"Yes please."

Grace's heart swelled when he did little things like that for her.

Every day since their beautiful simple wedding on the steps of Lombard Street, Grace's past had slipped further and further from her mind. In its place was a wonderful sense of now. Each moment shared with her handsome husband brought a peace that was abundantly filled with grace.

Grace Ruby patted the seat next to her. "Sit here with me." She was smiling a sly smile.

The one piece of furniture she just could not part with when she had her estate sale was her tête-a-tête settee. Michael and his son had dragged the heavy thing down from Grace's home in San Francisco and all the way up the stairs of the Bodega Bay home. They had teased her, saying that they both were going to need chiropractors for back adjustments.

The chair had so much meaning for Grace. It was the symbol of her alone time, as she kept everything away from the attached space. It was her perch as she watched life go by without participating. It was a spot for the first warm thing that she had allowed in... her kitten, BB.

The double, identical settee also was the source of her discovery of family. The chair represented the twins and finally spoke to her the truth. The chair was like family and Grace could never part with it.

Now her handsome husband sipped coffee from that attached seat every morning beside her.

"Here BB, here kitty," Michael called as the fat, fuzzy orange cat jumped up onto his lap and promptly curled up into a ball.

~

After the night on the cliff, Grace's self-imposed prison of guilt and regret had faded away. But Robin Rose had stayed tucked inside her heart.

Grace had soon started writing children's books about healing and strength. Azi did all of the art work and covers. Michael's grown daughter had loved the stories so much that she named her daughter Rosy after Robin Rose...and J after Grace's real mother, Jennifer, who had passed away in the early nineties.

The stories had revolved around Rachel working through life's problems with the help of her twin sister, Robin who was an angel. Azi's art work was amazing and, as a team, the sisters would collaborate the stories and art, all set in and around Muir Woods and the Pacific Ocean. Just like Grace's Lord Byron series, the Rachel and Robin books had sold out as soon as they hit the shelves.

Azi never married, but instead filled her creative spirit with art and her found family.

~

"Rosy J, it's time. Come on up," Azi called as she came out onto the porch, wiping paint off her hands with the corner of her apron.

"Just like you promised!" Rosy J cried, as she flew up the stairs and into the house.

Azi cleared the outdoor dining table and pulled up another chair.

"How about you, brother-in-law?" Azi teased.

"Oh no thank you, I'll sit this one out; can't disturb King BB."

Rosy J's parents were still asleep and Michael's son and daughter-in-law were taking a beach walk. The grandfolks were in charge.

"I'm back," the little redhead sang out as she held out a box in front of her.

"Here, let me help you with that," Grace offered as she got up from the settee and lifted Rosy J up to the table.

"Let's see how high we can go before we play the real game, okay everybody?" Rosy J shifted onto her knees.

Grace dumped out the antique Sidan blocks onto the table. She had saved the set with all of the words written on the blocks by her father.

"What does this say?" Grace asked Rosy J.

"R. O. S. E. Rose," the girl answered.

"And this?"

"R. U. B. Y. Ruby?"

"Yes, how about this?" Grace held up AZURE.

"I don't know. That one's hard," the little girl said, as she impatiently started stacking.

"That says, blue," Grace said as she winked at her beautiful sister.

"Okay," said Rosy J. "Love you lots."

"I love you too," Grace whispered, as she wrapped her hand around Rosy J's to help steady her as she built her tower; a tower of trust, filled with family, and grace.

THE END

Also available:
The Christmas Miracle Wrapped in Fur
Another book by Silver Lamb
Available on Amazon.com

Self Published in 2015

Made in the USA
Lexington, KY
21 March 2015